"You just have to

Nina looked at her friend Lizbeth, puzzled. "Lingo?"

"Yeah, take this ad," Lizbeth said, pointing to the magazine. "This guy wants someone who's 'commitment-minded' and 'independent.' That means you'd be willing to clean his apartment and you won't mind spending hours in a bar with his friends watching football on the big screen." Lizbeth ran her finger down the page. "All the rest of the stuff in this ad just means the guy will never remember to put the seat down. What you need is a man who enjoys golfing, sailing, theater and working out. That means he'll be self-employed, wealthy, intelligent and buff."

Nina shook her head, smiling. "Come on, they can't all be that bad. Here's one that looks pretty good. 'Friendly—'" she read.

"Horny."

"Likes to cuddle?"

"Wants sex," Lizbeth translated.

"So what's wrong with that?" Nina quipped. "At least I know we have something in common."

Dear Reader,

I've always loved to read the personal ads. Even though I've never answered one, as a single woman I've never given up hope that someday I might come across an ad that just cries out for a response. Perhaps a man from my past is looking for me, or maybe it will be one of those missed connections, where I meet a stranger's eyes across a crowded freeway.

That's where the idea behind THE PERSONAL TOUCH! came from—five different couples brought together through five very different personal ads. In *Mr. Right Now*, Nina Forrester still holds out hope that there's a Mr. Right just waiting for her. And if she isn't meant to meet him yet, she'll settle for Mr. Right Now. But when she meets dynamic Cameron Ryder, she soon finds out there's a third alternative—falling in love with Mr. Completely Wrong!

I hope you enjoy my twentieth Temptation novel. And to all my readers who've been with me since that very first book in 1993, a special thank-you for your support and enthusiasm.

All my best,

Kate Hoffmann

P.S. I love to hear from my readers. You can reach me c/o Harlequin Books, 225 Duncan Mill Road, Don Mills, Ontario, M3B 3K9, Canada.

Books by Kate Hoffmann

HARLEQUIN TEMPTATION

MR. RIGHT NOW
Kate Hoffmann

TORONTO • NEW YORK • LONDON
AMSTERDAM • PARIS • SYDNEY • HAMBURG
STOCKHOLM • ATHENS • TOKYO • MILAN • MADRID
PRAGUE • WARSAW • BUDAPEST • AUCKLAND

To Birgit Davis-Todd and Brenda Chin,
for their continued encouragement,
unerring instincts and editorial wisdom.

ISBN 0-373-25921-2

MR. RIGHT NOW

Copyright © 2001 by Peggy A. Hoffmann.

All rights reserved. Except for use in any review, the reproduction or
utilization of this work in whole or in part in any form by any electronic,
mechanical or other means, now known or hereafter invented, including
xerography, photocopying and recording, or in any information storage
or retrieval system, is forbidden without the written permission of the
publisher, Harlequin Enterprises Limited, 225 Duncan Mill Road,
Don Mills, Ontario, Canada M3B 3K9.

All characters in this book have no existence outside the imagination of
the author and have no relation whatsoever to anyone bearing the same
name or names. They are not even distantly inspired by any individual
known or unknown to the author, and all incidents are pure invention.

This edition published by arrangement with Harlequin Books S.A.

® and TM are trademarks of the publisher. Trademarks indicated with
® are registered in the United States Patent and Trademark Office, the
Canadian Trade Marks Office and in other countries.

Visit us at www.eHarlequin.com

Printed in U.S.A.

"I LIVE IN A CITY of seven million people. Three and a half million of them are men. Of those, there have to be at least a half million who are single. And out of those, there must be a few thousand who are decent guys."

Nina Forrester leaned over the counter and held her coffee mug under the stream of just-brewed coffee. When her mug was full, she shoved the pot back in its place and took a careful sip, moaning softly as the caffeine seeped into her bloodstream. Though she hadn't had a drop of wine all weekend, she had inhaled a two-pound bag of peanut M&Ms last night and the chocolate hangover was killing her. "Why can't I meet just one of those guys?"

"Bad weekend?" Lizbeth drawled, feigning sympathy.

Nina peered over the rim of the mug at her friend and co-worker, Lizbeth Gordon. Bad weekend? Not if crying through *Out of Africa* six times, gulping down handfuls of M&Ms, and waxing her bikini line qualified as bad. She'd had worse. There was that time she ate an entire frozen Sara Lee triple-layer fudge cake during the first hour of *Titanic*. And the Saturday she spent rearranging her underwear drawer, first by color, then by fabric, then by age. "I didn't even leave my apartment," Nina admitted. "And I'm starting to have sexual fantasies about the Chinese restaurant delivery man."

Lizbeth slipped her arm around Nina's shoulders and clucked her tongue. "Honey, don't you think it's about time you found yourself a nice stallion and went for a little ride? It's been a long time since you've visited the stable." From anyone else, the suggestion might have sounded ridiculous, but intoned in Lizbeth's lazy Southern accent, it sounded perfectly reasonable.

"What is it about you and horses?" Nina asked, pulling away and stalking out of the coffee room toward her office. "Last week you were telling me to get back in the saddle. When did Mr. Ed suddenly become your personal sex guru? According to you, *National Velvet* and *My Friend Flicka* are subversive sex manuals." She stopped at her office door. "Those were my favorite books when I was a kid," Nina said wistfully. "My life was all about horses. I didn't even look at boys."

"Huge, powerful, muscular, well-hung horses," Lizbeth said, fanning her face with her hand. "Gawd, I used to love those books, too." She giggled and pressed her fingers to her lips. "If Mama only knew she'd have burned them all."

Nina laughed. "You were perverse even back then!"

"And you were flat as a board and had a mouthful of braces." Lizbeth shuddered, tossing back her dark hair and smoothing her hands over her slender figure. "Admit it, you'd never want to go back to that time. Me? I was slightly chubby, a little shy and everything I wore was made of a petroleum by-product. It's a pure wonder I turned out as well as I did."

"Gee, and I thought you were born wearing a cashmere diaper and silk booties, dressed to seduce every boy baby in the nursery," Nina muttered.

If they hadn't been best friends, Nina was certain she'd hate Lizbeth. Any girl would. Lizbeth was stunningly beautiful. Nina was...cute. Lizbeth had three or four boyfriends dangling on any given day of the month, while the pints of Häagen-Dazs in Nina's freezer lasted longer than most of the men in her life.

And if personal humiliation wasn't enough, Nina had to face her professional inadequacies as well. As the lowly fact checker for *Attitudes* magazine, Nina spent most of her workday on the Internet or on the phone or at the library, checking the veracity of every article that passed through her office. Lizbeth had charmed her way into an assistant editor position in the fashion department. With *Attitudes'* profile as the hot magazine for twenty-somethings, that meant Lizbeth moved in circles that included wealthy designers and hot male models and handsome French photographers.

What's worse, she always looked like she'd stepped right out of a Calvin Klein ad, sleek and styled, smooth and sophisticated. Nina bought her clothes at vintage shops and thrift stores, favoring funky over fashionable. And the closest she got to styling her long blond hair was twisting it into a knot and securing it with a pencil or two.

But Lizbeth had one quality that made her an indispensable friend. No matter how bad Nina's life looked, all it took was one dry, but witty, comment from Lizbeth to put everything in perspective, to make Nina's worries dissolve into fits of laughter.

"You know what your problem is?" Lizbeth asked, following Nina into her tiny, windowless office.

"No, but I'm sure you're dying to tell me."

"You haven't had a date in almost six months. Honey, if you don't leave your apartment, how do you expect to meet anyone?" Lizbeth shook her head. "You're going to start to get...what do they call that? Angoraphobia?"

"Angoraphobia is a fear of fuzzy sweaters," Nina corrected. "Agoraphobia is a fear of strangers."

Lizbeth sighed. "The fact that you know something so obscure just proves my point," she said. "Since you broke up with that crazy drummer from that awful grunge band, you've had no life." She picked up a framed picture of Nina's nieces and stared at her reflection in the glass, fussing with her hair. "You know, if you're not married by the time you're thirty, chances are you'll never find a man."

"I'm only twenty-five!" Nina said.

"Five years can go by just like that," Lizbeth said, snapping her perfectly manicured fingers. "Besides, every year after age twenty-five is like dog years."

Nina didn't bother to ask for further explanation. Sometimes it was better just to let a few of them fly by. Instead, she picked up the latest issue of *Attitudes* and flipped through it. When she reached the back, her gaze fell on the pages of Personal Touch ads that ran every month. Men seeking women, women seeking men, men and women seeking something a little kinky.

"Maybe I should answer one of these ads," she murmured.

"Now there's an idea," Lizbeth said. "Not an idea *I'd* ever consider, but definitely an idea."

"Well, you don't have any trouble getting a date. And I know the ads work." Nina grabbed a file folder from her desk and opened it. "Look at these letters. Four couples who met through the Personal Touch ads this past year, and four marriages!"

"Where did you get those?"

"Eileen in customer service has been saving them for me. I'm thinking of pitching a story idea to Charlotte." She picked up one of the letters, this one from the mothers of the happy couple. "Nick Romano and Tyler Sheridan. Before Tyler met Nick, she was supposed to marry this other guy who ran out on their wedding and left her a 'Dear Joan' ad in our magazine. Nick, who's a P.I.—how sexy is that?—helped her track down her missing bridegroom and they fell in love. Have you ever heard of anything so romantic?"

"Oh, please. That sounds like one of those mushy romance novels!" Lizbeth said.

"Yes, it does. And I happen to love romance novels." Nina picked up another letter. "Here's one from Jane Dobson Warren. She placed a personal ad in *Attitudes* for her boss. He was looking for Holly Baskin, an old girlfriend. After Jane placed the ad, she got hit on the head, with a Cupid statue, no less. The concussion made her believe that *she* was Holly Baskin. And then she and her boss fell in love and got married." Nina sighed. "It *is* just like a romance novel, isn't it?"

"And you think those sweet little stories are going to

appeal to Charlotte?" Lizbeth shook her head. "You don't know Charlotte very well, do you."

Charlotte Danforth was publisher, editor, creative director, and sole stockholder of *Attitudes* magazine. She ran the publication like her own little fiefdom and she was the media queen. Her wealthy father's money had financed the magazine and though Charlotte couldn't edit her way out of a paper bag or balance a budget, she did have an uncanny knack for hiring talented people. And for spotting trends. And that's what *Attitudes* was all about—what's hot and what's not.

"I've got to do something to make Charlotte see me as assistant editor material," Nina said.

"Well, hon, that necklace won't help the cause. News flash—Wilma Flintstone isn't a fashion icon anymore."

Nina giggled and stuck out her tongue at Lizbeth as she slipped the letters back into the file. "I still think it's possible to find love through the personals. These four couples did." She picked up the magazine and began to scan the ads. "Here's a man that sounds nice. 'New York State of Mind. Good-looking professional seeks commitment-minded, independent SWF, 24-30. Enjoys motorcycles, the outdoors and NASCAR racing.' I love motorcycles."

Lizbeth snatched the magazine from Nina's fingers. "Allow me to translate, my naive little friend. Good-looking professional—decent-looking car salesman. Watch out when they say 'personable.' Then you can expect Quasimodo to show up at your front door."

"What about handsome?"

"Seriously deluded or completely self-absorbed."

"How do you know this? You have answered one of our ads!"

Lizbeth laughed lightly. "Don't be silly. Why would I need to answer an ad? I simply know men and their tendency to overstate their own virtues. You have to learn their lingo."

"Lingo?"

"Like this ad. 'Commitment-minded' means you'd be willing to clean his apartment. 'Independent' means you won't mind spending hours in a bar with his friends watching football on the big screen. And all the rest means the guy will never remember to put the toilet seat down." Lizbeth pointed to another ad. "'Enjoys gardening, antiquing, and cooking.' Mama's boy. What you need is a guy who enjoys golfing, sailing, theater and working out. That's means self-employed, wealthy, intelligent, and a great body."

"Here's one," Nina said. "Friendly—"

"Horny."

"Likes to cuddle?"

"Wants sex," Lizbeth translated.

"Loyal?" Nina asked.

"Obsessively jealous. The only thing worse is 'intense' which means 'stalker in training.' You'd be better off placing your own ad, honey. At least then you could screen the candidates."

"I don't know. Maybe I should just pitch the story about the four couples and their ads."

"It's a warm and fuzzy little story, but this isn't *Good Housekeeping*, Nina. *Attitudes* is edgy and trendy, and a little outrageous—not unlike that sweater you're wearing."

Nina glanced down at the vintage lime-green mohair with the Peter Pan collar. She bought it especially to go with the mod striped mini and green tights from the sixties. And the plastic bead necklace completed the look. "You don't think Charlotte would like it? The idea, not the sweater."

"If you want her to see you as an assistant editor, you're going to have to do more than pitch a story. You're going to have to go out there and experience the Personal Touch. Write your own ad, go on a few dates and tell your story. And the more horrible the experience, the better."

"I wouldn't know what to say in an ad," Nina replied. "How do I advertise for Mr. Right?"

Lizbeth sighed dramatically, then searched the surface of Nina's desk until she found a pad of paper. "Honey, you don't have time to look for Mr. Right. You're looking for Mr. Right Now. Mr. Right This Minute. Charlotte's been interviewing for an editorial assistant for the past month. If you get this story done and turn it in, maybe she'll give you the job."

"All right," Nina said. "I'll do it."

"All right," Lizbeth repeated.

"Nancy!"

Nina and Lizbeth looked up to find Charlotte Danforth standing at the doorway of Nina's office. As always, she looked like she'd just tumbled out of bed, though this morning she wore evening clothes, a sexy beaded designer number that probably cost more than Nina made in a year. It was clear Charlotte hadn't been to bed at all, but came right to work from whatever party she'd attended the night before. Her hair was

mussed and she puffed incessantly on a French cigarette. Yet even in such disarray, she was still a force of
nature, a human hurricane that left workers weeping
in her path.

"Nina," Nina corrected.

Charlotte sniffed, then shrugged. "Yes, fine, all right,
Nina. I need you to check a fact for me. I need to know
what the trendiest spot on the body is for a rather small
tattoo. And the most popular subject matter. Check for
both men and women, I'm sure it's different. And give
me a breakdown by age if you can."

"Charlotte, I'm not sure there have ever been any
studies done on—"

"I don't care if there haven't been studies, Nora!"

"Nina," she reminded. "Is this for an article? Because we did a story on tattoos just a few months ago."

"I just need the information, Nola," Charlotte
snapped. "It's personal. By the end of the day?"

With that, she turned and hurried from the door,
leaving Nina to wonder how she'd ever convince
Charlotte to give her an editorial position if the woman
couldn't even remember her name. "Oh, sure. I'll just
call the Census Bureau. I'm sure I remember answer-
ing the tattoo question on the 2000 census. Right hip,
tiny rose." She tossed aside the personal ads and
straightened her desk. "I guess I'm going to be spending the rest of the day on the phone talking to tattoo
parlors," Nina murmured.

Lizbeth smiled. "And I'd guess that Charlotte got
herself drunk last night and ended up in one of those
24-hour tattoo parlors in the East Village. And now she
wants *you* to tell her that she didn't make a big fashion

faux pas getting that big old butterfly tattooed on her butt."

Nina's eyes went wide. "Really?" At least when Nina had decided on a tattoo she'd been sober and possessed of good taste, ending up with a tiny flower on a spot that only showed when she wore a bikini.

"As long as whatever she got is on the top of the list, hon, you'll make her happy."

"But how am I supposed to know?"

Lizbeth stood and smoothed her skirt. "Leave it to me. She's bound to tell someone what she did last night. She always blabs when she's got a hangover. Five minutes later, it will be all over the office. I'll feed you the facts and you make up the research."

"But that wouldn't be ethical," Nina protested.

"Honey, you do want the job in editorial, don't you?"

Nina nodded hesitantly. "Yes, I do. And while you're finding out about Charlotte's new tattoo, I'm going to work on my ad. Even if it doesn't result in a great story, at least I'll have something better to do on a Saturday night than polishing my shoes and fishing spare change out of the sofa."

"That's the spirit!" her friend cried. "Get on that pony and ride! Yee-hah!"

Nina smiled at Lizbeth. "And maybe, if I'm very lucky, I'll find Mr. Right. And if not him, then Mr. Right Now."

THE AFTER-WORK CROWD HAD settled in at Jitterbug's, the coffee shop across the street from *Attitudes'* Soho headquarters. It was a favorite spot for the staff who gathered regularly to sip lattes and mochas and discuss whatever outrageous request Charlotte Danforth had thrown their way during the day. But Nina had more important things on her mind than commiserating about her quirky and unpredictable boss. Nagging little projects had occupied nearly every minute of her workday and she hadn't had a single moment to get back to her ad for the Personal Touch.

Nina found her regular table in the corner and tossed her coat over the back of her chair, then dropped her bag on the smooth marble tabletop. She glanced over at the counter and waved at Martha who nodded, a silent agreement to make Nina's usual—a double skinny decaf latte with a shot of hazelnut. She sat down and spread her work out in front of her—the Personal Touch ads from the last four weeks, her notepad, personalized with her name and the name of the magazine emblazoned across the bottom, and a pencil with a brand new eraser. She'd also brought a list of attributes she'd quickly compiled for Mr. Right during her lunch hour.

"Cute, considerate, humorous, spontaneous," she read out loud. "Nice hair, kind eyes, and—"

"A fluffy tail and good teeth. Honey, you sound like you're advertising for a Pomeranian, not a man. If I were you, I'd stick with the man. He won't poop on the rug." Lizbeth flopped down in the chair across from Nina's and sighed dramatically. "You won't believe the day I've had. They sent me size two samples and size six models. Thank God for duct tape. We cut the back seams open and taped the clothes on."

Nina forced a sympathetic smile. She really wasn't in

the mood to hear Lizbeth's tale of woe. She'd hoped to spend some time on her own, sipping coffee and carefully composing her ad. It had to be just right and it would take a lot of thought. "I'm just starting on this," she murmured.

"So, what do you have so far?" Lizbeth asked.

"Actually...nothing."

Lizbeth sighed and shook her head. She pointed to Nina's pad. "Take this down." She paused for a moment, then smiled. "Headline—Looking for Mr. Right Now." She glanced over at Nina and frowned. "I said, take this down." Nina scribbled as Lizbeth spoke. "Attractive, fun-loving, energetic SWF, 25, seeks adventurous Adonis, 25-35, for wild Saturday nights and lazy Sunday afternoons."

"Don't you think that last part makes me sound a little...loose?"

"Honey, the whole thing makes you sound loose. That's the point. What do you think I mean by 'fun-loving' and 'energetic'? Likes sex and likes it all the time." Lizbeth gave her a long look. "You want someone to answer the ad, don't you?"

Frowning, Nina ripped the top sheet off and crumpled it in her fist, then noticed Martha waving in her direction. "I'll write my own ad, thank you very much." She pushed back from the tiny table to retrieve her coffee, fully intending to toss Lizbeth's ad in the garbage.

But as she paid Martha, she contemplated her friend's strategy. Time was running out. Maybe she ought to put off her search for Mr. Right and concentrate on Mr. Right Now. And kissing a few frogs made a lot better copy than finding Prince Charming on the first time out. Nina opened her fist and dropped the wad of paper on the counter, then smoothed it out. She re-read the words as she grabbed her coffee. With a soft sigh, she turned and started back toward her table, making mental edits to the text. She didn't have to sound like a trollop, did she?

She didn't notice the man who stepped into her path, but in the blink of an eye, he was there. With a soft cry of surprise, she ran face first into a tall, broad-shouldered figure. Her coffee mug tipped between them, spilling hot coffee all over his wide chest, his flat belly and his...lap.

The man jumped back, cursing softly as he brushed the steaming liquid from his finely tailored shirt, his startled gaze taking in the coffee-soaked fabric. It was only then that Nina got a good look at his face. Her breath caught in her throat and, for a moment, she was unable to speak. "Adventurous Adonis," she murmured.

Even wincing in pain, she could see what a handsome man he was—strong features, a chiseled mouth and vivid green eyes. For a long moment, she couldn't speak. Then the words began tumbling out of her mouth. "Oh—oh, dear. I'm so sorry. I—I didn't see— and when you stepped in front—that's probably a very expensive—are you all right—I didn't—"

"I'm fine," he muttered, plucking at the soaked fabric of his dress shirt and silk tie. "It's my fault. I wasn't paying attention."

Nina reached over his table and grabbed the napkin dispenser, then tugged out a wad of napkins. But as she spun around to hand them to the man, she knocked over the tall mug of coffee on his table. It tumbled to the floor and splashed onto his shiny dress loafers. Half the napkins fluttered to the floor and Nina bent down to pick them up before attempting to wipe the coffee off his shoes. Good grief, he even had handsome feet.

When she glanced up at him, she caught him smiling sardonically. "I don't think I've got any coffee on my left pant leg," he said. "Maybe you'd like to order another cup and finish the job?"

"I'll just get you cleaned up and then—" She reached up and dabbed frantically at the front of his pants, then realized where she was dabbing and groaned softly. "I—I guess you should probably do that area on your own." What was she thinking? Nina glanced around to see the entire clientele of Jitterbug's watching her with amusement. What were *they* thinking?

He grabbed her elbow, pulling her to her feet. Afraid to look up, Nina halfheartedly wiped at his shirt with the sheet of paper she had clutched in her other hand. When he took it from her fingers and shoved it in his pants pocket, she had no choice but to meet his gaze. An apologetic smile twitched at her lips and she risked a look up. "I—I'm sorry. Sometimes, I'm so clumsy. Are you all right?"

"I'm fine," he murmured, his gaze fixed on hers for the first time. "And there's no need to apologize. It was partly my fault, too."

She'd never seen a greener pair of eyes in her life. Or a sexier smile. Or a straighter nose. Or a— Nina swallowed hard. "But your shirt. It's ruined."

He chuckled dryly. "I never liked this shirt. Gives me a good excuse to toss it."

For a long moment, they didn't speak. Nina tried to remember if she'd apologized, but she couldn't recall exactly what she'd said to him. Maybe it was the eyes, the penetrating eyes that seemed to send every rational thought running from her mind. Or the lips that looked like they'd been made especially to kiss women, and lots of them. Even the faint stubble of a beard was more than she could bear.

Was this one of those men she'd been wondering about, the one in a million and a half, the last single decent guy in all of New York City? She glanced at his left hand, looking for the telltale wedding band. There was none. Oh, if he was the one in a million, she'd certainly made a mess of destiny! "Can—can I buy you another coffee?" she offered.

He shook his head, his gaze never wavering from hers. "I was just leaving. I've got a meeting."

Her breath caught again and she waited for him to step away, to walk out the door and out of her life forever. For all she knew, she'd just dumped coffee all over Mr. Right and now he was going to just disappear without another word. "Of course," she murmured. "And look at what I've done."

He glanced over his shoulder and winced. "I really have to go." He grabbed his suit jacket and briefcase from a chair, then slowly turned and started toward the door. Nina took one step to stop him, but then she noticed the rest of the patrons still watching her.

"I really am sorry," she called as the door swung shut behind him. "A little cold water and a good nonchlorine bleach will get that stain right out!" She looked around the coffee shop, frowning. "Show's over. You can all go back to your coffee," she muttered.

With a flush of embarrassment, she hurried back to her table and sat down. "Was that as bad as I think it was?" Nina murmured. "Did I make a total fool of myself? And was there anyone in this place who didn't hear me giving him laundry advice?"

Lizbeth reached over and patted her hand excitedly. "That was absolutely perfect!" she cried. "Honey, I didn't think you had it in you, but that move was pure brilliance!"

"What move?"

"Spilling coffee all over that stunningly gorgeous man. I don't even think I would have had the courage to do something so outrageous, especially when he had on a handmade French shirt. Those things cost five hundred apiece if they cost a penny."

"Really?" Nina squeaked. "Five hundred dollars?"

"Couldn't you tell? Oh, honey, the way it hugged his body and nipped in around that waist. It fit him like a second skin. That kind of shirt makes a girl wonder what's underneath. Every woman in this place was pea-green with envy of you."

"It was an accident," Nina said numbly.

Lizbeth gave her a sly look. "Oh, please. You expect me to believe that? So, did you give him your phone number? You know, offer to pay his cleaning bill? Buy him a new shirt?"

"No. He didn't ask that I pay." Nina frowned and looked over at the door. "He said he was going to throw the shirt out. I guess I should have offered. But it was his fault, too."

"You didn't give him your phone number," Lizbeth stated, her voice flat and laced with disbelief. "Please tell me you at least got his name. Or you gave him yours."

Nina covered her face with her hands. "No. I just couldn't think. I mean, there he was, all covered with coffee. And there I was," she moaned, "rubbing his crotch with napkins." She moaned again, this time with more emphasis. "I really screwed that up. For a second, I thought it might be destiny, but then he looked at me and my mind just went haywire and my knees went all wobbly." Nina peered at Lizbeth through her fingers. "He probably wasn't my type anyway, right? I mean, he was wearing a suit and I never go for businessmen. And he seemed a little up-tight." She drew a shaky breath. "And a guy who wears five-hundred dollar shirts is way out of my league. I'm sure it would never have worked out."

Lizbeth pushed to her feet, shaking her head. "Did you bother to look at the man? He's *every* woman's type! Nuns would lust after the guy." She grabbed her purse and slung it over her shoulder, then wagged her finger at Nina. "Maybe you should place that ad. It's clear that you don't have a chance of getting a gorgeous man the regular way—by trickery and manipulation. I have to go, I have a date. But I want you to sit here and think about what you did wrong. We'll discuss it later."

Nina nodded dejectedly, like a child chastised. "I don't think I'll be able to put it out of my mind."

"I'll call you." Lizbeth turned on her heel and walked toward the door. When it closed behind her, Nina busied herself with picking up her belongings. She grabbed the pad of paper and started to shove it in her bag, but decided against it. Snatching up her pencil, she closed her eyes for a moment, then began to write.

"Coffee Collision," she murmured, writing the words out in capital letters. "Jitterbug's in Manhattan, March 15th. My latte met your shirt. Call me."

Nina stared down at the text. Did she really have the courage to place the ad? Chances were remote at best that he'd see it. After all, he wasn't the typical *Attitudes* reader. With a soft oath, she ripped the page off the pad. But instead of crumpling it in her hand, she carefully folded it and placed it in her jacket pocket.

"Forget the guy. You're not looking for Mr. Right, you're looking for Mr. Right Now—he's the man who will get you a job in editorial."

But as Nina tried to compose another ad, she couldn't keep her mind on the task at hand. Her thoughts kept wandering back to the man in the coffee-stained shirt, to the firm set of his mouth when he smiled, to the strong grasp of his fingers on her elbow, to the tremor that raced through her arm and made her head swim the moment he'd touched her.

She'd never believed in instant attraction, but that was only because she'd never experienced it before. Now that she had, Nina wanted to experience it again. She'd just have to find a way to make it happen.

"WHAT HAPPENED TO YOU?"

Cameron Ryder stood on the sidewalk outside the

coffee shop. He glanced down at his ruined shirt and tie and shrugged. "A little accident with a cup of coffee...and some crazy woman."

He looked back over his shoulder. A beautiful, bewitching, crazy woman, he added silently. Now that he'd put a little distance between them, he wasn't quite sure what to think of her. She hadn't really been a woman at all, at least not the kind of sophisticated and overtly sexy woman he usually socialized with. She was sweet and slightly goofy, more a girl than woman. She'd been dressed a little oddly, in a hairy chartreuse sweater and a short little skirt that showed off shapely legs.

His mind conjured an image of her, her startling blue eyes and her golden blond hair twisted into a knot with spikes sticking out all over the place. He frowned— and chartreuse legs. In truth, she'd looked like one of those bohemian girls who spent her days and nights in Soho coffee bars and art galleries, smoking cigarettes and quoting Sartre.

Still, he couldn't deny the current of attraction that had raced through his body the instant their eyes met, the warmth that seeped through his bloodstream when he touched her, the flood of amusement that made him smile when she so earnestly wiped off the front of his trousers.

Unlike most of the women he'd known, this woman lacked the hard, cynical edge that came from living in Manhattan. Her eyes were wide and clear blue, almost innocent. And she had a fresh, unpretentious look about her, unmarred by overdone cosmetics. With any other woman, he might have suspected she dumped the coffee on purpose. But the look of sheer surprise and mortification on her pretty face was enough to tell him differently. Cam laughed softly and shook his head. Good grief, he'd barely been able to get out a word or two, looking into those eyes.

What was this instant fascination he had with a complete stranger? Maybe he'd been working too hard lately. He hadn't had much time for a social life and any woman would appear attractive to a man who hadn't bothered with dating in the past few months. He fought the urge to walk back inside for just one more look, but then Jeff cleared his throat and pointed to his watch.

"We've got a half hour before we meet with Charlotte Danforth," he said. "There's probably time to run back to your apartment and change."

Ever the organized businessman, Jeff Myers was chief operating officer of Cameron's company, NightRyder. Jeff had been a fellow college student when, ten years ago, Cam had created the Internet site for Gen X entertainment and night life. He'd been there when the company moved from dorm room to apartment to office complex across the river in Jersey. And he'd been there at their stock offering, when the IPO turned Jeff's thirty-percent interest into millions of dollars in just a few hours.

"I don't need to change," Cam said. Though he might be able to make the trip uptown and back to his Riverside Drive apartment, he had no intention of doing so. "I'm not going to the meeting. You're my partner and you have my complete trust and authority. I want you to present the offer."

Cam had been working toward this acquisition for as long as he could remember and now that it was time to make his move, he preferred to stand back and watch. Five years ago, *Attitudes* was barely a blip on the media radar. No one expected it to succeed, especially with socialite-party-girl Charlotte Danforth at the helm. But her rich daddy was willing to pay a price to get his little girl into the work world and out of his hair. Charles Danforth, one of New York's wealthiest men, was the magazine's only investor. Even the headquarters of *Attitudes* was housed in a Danforth building, probably rent-free.

"I don't know why you want the magazine," Jeff Myers murmured. "With all the money the old man has pumped into it, we have no idea what it's really worth. She's probably never had to prepare a financial statement, so we're buying blind. Why not buy something else?"

Cameron shrugged. "Well, *Rolling Stone* would be too expensive. So would *Premiere* and *Entertainment*. *Attitudes* is a weekly, it's a trend-setter, and their subscription list fits our demographic. It's a good match for us," he said. "And I don't care what it costs. I want the magazine and I want you to do everything necessary to get it."

He smiled to himself. It felt good to say that, to know that when it came to a business acquisition, money was no longer an object. There was a time not so long ago that he'd struggled to make ends meet. He'd just founded NightRyder, and though hip and trendy New

Yorkers visited the site to learn all the latest on movies, music, and entertainment, the Internet was still young. Every penny he'd saved, most of it earmarked for his last year at NYU, had gone into the design. Four years later, when NightRyder had become the most popular Internet site nationwide in the 20- to 30-year-old demographic, the advertisers started coming and Cam's life as an Internet entrepreneur began.

"Don't you think you're carrying this mystery man thing a little too far?" Jeff asked. "You're making too much money to keep your face out of the public eye forever. And you're the Ryder in NightRyder, Cam. You should be there when we make our offer and Charlotte Danforth accepts."

Cam chuckled. "She's not going to accept."

"What? But she has to. We've done our research. Daddy Danforth is just about ready to cut her off, if he hasn't already. Her creditors are hounding her. And she's spending more and more time partying with her high society friends than running her magazine. The time is right."

"She's not going to accept," Cam insisted. "*Attitudes* is her baby. Besides, we're only going to offer her half what we think the magazine is worth."

"But I thought we decided—"

"I know what we decided. But I changed my mind. I need some more information before we make a solid offer."

"Cam, it's a privately held publication. I don't think she's going to open up the books and let us browse before we talk money."

"I know. But we can afford to wait her out, until

she's a little more desperate. And while we do that, maybe we can get some inside information."

Jeff nodded. "I suppose that wouldn't be a bad idea. Charlotte Danforth has hired and fired enough people. We could always find a disgruntled employee who might want to talk."

"Then do it," he said. "And call me after your meeting with Danforth. I want a full report."

Jeff nodded, then started across the street. Cameron watched as he walked in the front entrance of the ornate cast-iron building, one of the many that lined the streets in this section of Soho. Then he turned and shoved his hands in his pockets, warming them in the chilly evening air.

His fingers toyed with a wad of paper in his pocket and he pulled it out, only to find the crumpled sheet the beautiful girl had used on his shirt, the scribblings on it now blurred by the coffee. Part of the paper was still completely legible—the *Attitudes* logo across the bottom and the name on the top.

"From the desk of Nina Forrester," he murmured. "Nina." The name seemed to suit her, light, airy, a name that sounded like a peal of laughter or a twinkle in the eye. "So that's her name."

It took a few moments for the importance of his discovery to sink in. Nina Forrester worked at *Attitudes!* And he was looking for someone on the inside, someone to give him insight into the mercurial Charlotte Danforth and the state of her business affairs. His mind instantly began to form a strategy.

Why not go back inside and join her? He could engage her in conversation, bring up the subject of work.

Most women loved to talk about their work, especially to a man who appeared interested in what she had to say. But the thought of manipulating her for his own purposes rankled.

Though rising to the top of the Internet world had taken immense technical knowledge, staying on top required a fair bit of ruthlessness. Still, he'd never deliberately deceived anyone to get what he wanted. Wasn't that what he was considering now? He held the paper up to read the rest of the scribbling in the waning light of day, wondering what she'd been working on.

"Looking for Mr. Right Now?" he read, confusion wrinkling his brow. "Attractive, fun-loving, energetic SWF, 25, seeks adventurous Adonis, 25-35, for wild Saturday nights and lazy Sunday afternoons."

Cameron reread the words again, simply to assure himself that he'd read them right the first time. "Adventurous Adonis? Wild Saturday nights and lazy Sunday afternoons?"

Usually, he was an excellent judge of character, able to detect hidden agendas and ulterior motives in a single glance. But if Nina Forrester had written this ad, then he'd been completely fooled by her innocent smile. A woman who enjoyed wild Saturday nights and lazy Sunday afternoons would probably have no qualms about dumping her coffee on a single guy sitting in a coffee shop. Maybe he'd been too hasty in his earlier impression. Perhaps she might be able to help him get inside *Attitudes* magazine.

Cameron started back down the street toward the subway stop, carefully folding the paper as he walked. He'd never really thought of himself as an Adonis—far from it. Up until he made his first million, he was just a computer geek, the kid with the thick glasses and the pocketful of pens, the president of the computer club and the chess club, a guy girls did their best to ignore.

Funny how a little power and money seemed to change him in others' eyes. It always took him unawares, for inside, there was still a tiny bit of the geek left. He'd simply gotten a few years older, so that grown-up muscle now covered his once bony body. An uptown haircut and designer clothing had completed the transformation in his outward appearance. Maybe money did make the man.

He turned and stared back at the sidewalk in front of the coffee shop. Though his curiosity was piqued, he wasn't about to go back inside. He knew her name, where she worked, and where she played. He could find her if he needed to.

"Better to wait," he murmured with a chuckle. "After all, no self-respecting Adonis would be seen with a huge coffee stain on his chest."

2

"HURRY UP! Staff meeting in the conference room. Charlotte wants everyone there."

Nina looked up at Lizbeth from the reference books spread across her desk. She'd been caught up in finding out the name of the original designer of platform shoes and had lost all track of time. Before that, she'd been immersed in an idle contemplation of the mystery man she'd spilled coffee on last night. She still couldn't put him out of her mind, going over every stupid mistake she'd made.

Why hadn't she offered to send his shirt to the cleaner or pay for a new shirt? Why hadn't she given him her phone number or at least introduced herself? Nina had lived in Manhattan for seven years, since her college days at Columbia, and she'd never met a man quite as handsome as the man she'd affectionately dubbed "Coffee Man."

A more appropriate name would come to her, but Nina was already certain that this man would occupy her fantasies for a long time to come. Besides being incredibly handsome, he was funny and smart and confident, though how she knew all these things she wasn't sure. What she did know was that if she ever saw him again she wasn't going to let him get away a second time.

"Nina?"

With a start, Nina glanced up at Lizbeth, drawn from her daydream. "Oh, right. The meeting." She reached up and raked her fingers through her hair. Though Lizbeth looked like she'd just stepped out of a magazine ad, Nina usually managed to run a comb through her hair on the way down her apartment stairs and dash on mascara and a little lipstick during her bus ride from her East Village apartment. "She wants everyone there?" she asked.

"Big news," Lizbeth warned. "I think bad news, too, from the look on Charlotte's face. She's wearing the same clothes she had on yesterday afternoon, her hair is a mess and she's got raccoon eyes from her mascara. I don't think I've ever seen Charlotte looking like a roadside rodent. Maybe Daddy Danforth has finally cut the purse strings."

Nina's heart twisted in her chest. If the magazine was having financial problems then the first jobs to be cut would be editorial assistants. Her current position as fact checker was safe as long as *Attitudes* was still publishing. But her future as an assistant editor with the magazine suddenly looked bleak. "Are you sure she wants me there? I'm never invited to staff meetings."

"She specifically asked that you come," Lizbeth said.

Nina jumped to her feet, hope springing to life inside her. "Did she ask for me by name?"

"Yes," Lizbeth said. "She walked in my office, told me about the meeting and requested that I be sure to tell Tina."

Nina rolled her eyes and cursed softly. "Is my name

that hard to remember? I've worked for Charlotte for nearly three years! She sees me at least four or five times a week." She looked down at the bottle-green satin Chinese jacket and flowered skirt she wore. "I don't look like I blend into the furniture, do I?"

Lizbeth considered Nina's skirt for a few seconds and put on her best Southern drawl. "My mama did have some dining room portieres that looked a lot like your skirt."

Nina strode to the door, pinching Lizbeth's arm as she passed. "You're so mean to me. I don't know why you're still my friend."

Lizbeth fell into step beside her as they strolled toward the conference room. "Because I'm the only one who really appreciates you," she said with a lazy smile. "And your whimsical fashion sense." She gave her the once-over with her critical fashion eye. "All right, I love the jacket. There, are you happy?"

One thing Nina was happy about was that Lizbeth had forgotten the events of the night before. The last thing she needed was her best friend chiding her about the mistakes she'd made. Lizbeth just didn't understand. She'd always had boys fawning over her and men falling at her feet. Nina had discovered boys a little later in life, so she'd been playing catch-up since she was eighteen. She sighed softly, glancing at Lizbeth. No matter how long she worked at it, she'd never catch up to Lizbeth.

By the time they reached the conference room, all the chairs had been taken by senior staff. Lizbeth and Nina stood against the back wall and watched as Charlotte called the meeting to order. Nina couldn't recall ever attending a staff meeting before. Charlotte preferred to deal with her one-on-one and important news was usually passed on to Nina through office gossip, haphazard memos, or not at all.

"We have a problem," Charlotte began. "A huge problem. I've called you all in here because, frankly, I don't know what to do." To Nina's surprise, the normally icy Charlotte looked like she was about to cry. "I can't go to Daddy, so I'm asking all of you for your help." She sniffed. "I know I haven't always been the nicest boss, but I can't change that now." Her voice trembled slightly. "Yesterday evening I had a visit from a representative of NightRyder, some Internet company with truckloads of cash. They offered to buy the magazine."

A collective gasp sounded in the silence of the conference room, followed by a low murmur of whispered comments. Lizbeth turned to look at Nina, her eyes wide.

Charlotte ran her fingers through her mussed hair and Nina noticed the shadows beneath her boss's eyes. She had been crying. "Don't worry, the offer wasn't good enough to accept. But the next one might be. And as you all know, this magazine has always operated on a...tight budget. And now that Daddy—I mean, now that my investors have decided to curtail their rather generous funding, the magazine is more vulnerable than ever. We have to tighten our belt, be more efficient and—and do all those other things you people do when we need to save money. I'm sure you know what they are."

"Like cutting back on expensive business lunches at

the city's best restaurants?" Lizbeth murmured. "And throwing lavish parties for male models then writing them off against our photo budgets?"

"Shhh!" Nina hissed.

"Lena, where are you?" Charlotte demanded. Her gaze searched the room, but no one spoke up. The rest of the employees glanced nervously back and forth. "Well, where is my head of research? Lizbeth, I told you to bring her along. Where is Lena?"

Suddenly Nina realized that Charlotte was talking to her. She raised her hand nervously. "I'm here," she said. "Tina, I—I mean, Nina. Nina Forrester." She groaned inwardly and bit back a curse. Now *she* couldn't even remember her own name!

"Tina, I want you to find out everything you can about this NightRyder company. It's owned by someone named Cameron Ryder. Call whoever you call and get me something, anything, on this man. I need to know everything I can about the enemy before I face him again. Oh, and find out if he's married." She glanced around the room. "As for the rest of you, no more spending. Cultivate new vendors who will extend us credit. Sell more ad pages. And there'll be no more free beverages in the coffee room!"

With that, she swept out of the room, leaving her staff to wonder whether they might be better off with Cameron Ryder at the helm of *Attitudes*. Nina and Lizbeth hurried out in front of the crowd, anxious to regain the privacy of Nina's office. When they closed the door behind them, they both gasped and gaped at each other.

"I suppose we ought to start revising our résumés," Nina said.

"You don't actually think Charlotte will sell to this NightRyder guy, do you?"

Nina shook her head. "She's not much of a business-woman and the magazine has always struggled. But then, maybe this Ryder isn't much of a businessman." She reached for her computer keyboard, then looked at the screen. The moment she'd walked in that morning, she'd typed up her two ads—the "coffee collision" ad for Mr. Right and the "Adonis" ad for Mr. Right Now, still torn between which one to place.

As she stared at the screen, Nina's mind again wandered back to her encounter with "Coffee Man." How many times had she brushed him from her thoughts, trying to convince herself there was probably some-thing seriously wrong with him? Maybe he picked his teeth or burped after dinner. Maybe he hated modern art or detested the theater. He could have all sorts of disgusting flaws. Like all the other men she'd met, she'd probably have dropped him sooner or later, so what was the point even wasting brain cells on him?

A soft moan slipped from her lips. But he was in-credibly intriguing. She suspected he had a body to match that gorgeous face, hidden beneath his staid at-tire. And though she usually didn't go for the suit-and-tie type, he wouldn't always be wearing clothes. A de-licious shiver skittered up her spine and she couldn't help but smile.

"Well? What have you found?"

Nina blinked, then glanced up at Lizbeth. "What? Oh, nothing. It'll take more than a few seconds." She shook her head and turned back to the monitor, hoping to hide the warm flush that had crept up her cheeks. "But I'll let you know as soon as I do," she murmured, closing the document that held the two ads.

Lizbeth started toward the door. "Good luck," she said, the usual light and teasing tone now gone from her voice. "All of us are counting on you."

She closed the door behind her, leaving Nina to her own thoughts. Though the business with Cameron Ryder was urgent, she allowed herself just a few more moments to think about her fantasy man. Maybe if she finished up her research for Charlotte early, she'd go back to the coffee shop after work. Perhaps, he'd be there, hoping that she might return as well.

And this time, she wouldn't be such a dope. She'd catch his eye from across the room. And then she'd smile, a hesitant, but coy smile, with maybe a hint of surprise. Then a little wave, playful but not too aggressive. After all, she didn't want him to think she'd come looking for him on purpose. No, it was best to play hard to get—but not *too* hard to get.

"So how do I do that?"

She glanced down at what she'd pulled from her closet that morning. It wasn't exactly conservative, but she thought it was pretty. "Maybe Mr. Right goes for the kind of woman who wears conservative clothes and spends more than a few minutes making herself look pretty in the morning," she murmured, worrying over a loose thread on her jacket. She tugged on it and a button went flying across the room.

Yeah, she was smooth all right. For all she knew, Mr. Right might have a Ms. Right waiting at home, someone beautiful and sophisticated. He might even be married! Not every man wore a wedding band. Since last night, she'd spun a whole fantasy around this guy, giving him qualities she wasn't even sure he'd possessed.

"This is ridiculous," Nina said. "Your social life is so bad that you've been reduced to dreaming up a relationship with a complete stranger, turning a few minutes at Jitterbug's into two kids, a dog and a three-bedroom house in Jersey."

With a soft oath, she brought up the computer screen that held her two ads. Pounding furiously on the Delete key, she erased her "Coffee Collision" ad. It was time to stop dreaming and take control of her life. Mr. Right was a silly fantasy. And Mr. Right Now would have to wait until after this crisis with NightRyder was solved. For the next few days, she'd have to focus all her time and energy on just one man—the mysterious and very dangerous Cameron Ryder.

THE MARCH WEATHER had turned brisk again, a cold, damp wind swirling around the city and smelling of a late season snow. Cameron pulled his leather jacket closed as he stepped out of the cab in front of the coffee shop. He stood for a long moment on the sidewalk, trying to decide whether to venture inside. The windows were fogged and the sound of music drifted out every time the door was opened, but he waited.

He wasn't really sure why he'd come. He'd already decided not to use Nina Forrester for information about *Attitudes* magazine. Too many complications. Yet, he had still made a simple phone call to the magazine and learned she was a fact checker, a job that probably didn't put her in daily contact with the editor and publisher, Charlotte Danforth, anyway. The information she might be able to provide would be marginally valuable at best—or that's what he chose to tell himself.

"So why the hell am I here?" Cameron muttered.

Was it curiosity? He couldn't deny that he'd found their little encounter over a cup of coffee surprisingly intriguing. Maybe it was the contradiction, the wide-eyed naif hiding a provocative siren. He reached into his jacket pocket and withdrew the ad she'd written. If he hadn't taken it from her hand, he never would have put the two together. But then, he'd never been a very astute judge of the female mind. For a guy who didn't have a real date until he was a junior in college, Cameron Ryder had been forced to learn fast, leaving several very pronounced gaps in his studies.

There had been women, a fair number of them since he'd started NightRyder, but never anything serious. He thought back to his days in college, to the fantasies of beautiful, sexy women, blond and leggy, with tanned and trainer-toned bodies. They were every misfit's dream and over the past five years he'd dated—and bedded—a string of them.

But somehow, the reality had never lived up to the fantasy. Though many of the women were nice enough, there was nothing beyond the gorgeous bodies except the desire to capture a wealthy and powerful man. More and more, he'd found himself playing the role they'd wanted to him play, pretending to be someone he could never be, smooth and sophisticated, yet caught in a series of empty relationships.

So he'd stopped dating months ago, instead putting his energy back into the business. Nina Forrester was the first woman he'd found even remotely interesting in all that time. He exhaled, his breath clouding in front of his face, then pulled the door open. He hadn't been inside more than a few moments before he saw her. She was sitting at a table over in the corner. She turned to look at some papers she'd spread in front of her and he silently studied her profile—the pretty nose, the lush lips, the golden hair that framed her face in soft tendrils.

Without thinking, he crossed the room and came to a stop beside her table. Suddenly, he wasn't quite sure what to say. He felt as if he'd been transported back to that awful moment in high school when he'd worked up the nerve to ask the prettiest cheerleader out on a date, only to have her laugh in his face.

Cameron swallowed hard. "I owe you a cup of coffee."

She looked up and for an instant, he thought he saw delight in her pretty blue eyes and a tiny trace of a smile curling her lips. "Hi," she said, her voice breathless with surprise. She stood up quickly, knocking her hip against the table and nearly spilling her cup of coffee in the process. "What are you doing here?"

Cameron knew enough about women to play it cool. "I was just passing by and thought I'd give the coffee another try."

"Oh, right," she said, a nervous twitch of her lips passing for a smile. "I guess you didn't get much of a taste of it last night." She paused. "I should buy you a cup." She motioned to the second chair at her table. "Why don't you sit down." Without another word, she hurried off. But a few seconds later, she returned, her face colored with a pretty blush. "How do take your coffee?" she asked.

"With just a little cream," Cameron replied, slipping out of his jacket. He watched her return to the counter, then sat down and waited. When she came back with his coffee, he stood and pulled out her chair. But as she sat down, she caught her elbow on his arm and half the coffee spilled all over her papers.

"Oh, no!" she cried.

Cameron grabbed the cup from her hand just as it was about to dump all over his sleeve, then set it down. He handed her a stack of napkins. "You are a menace with a cup of coffee," he teased. "Maybe we should stick to tea."

Nina mopped up the coffee on her side of the table, then glanced up at him, gracing him with one of the most beautiful smiles he'd ever seen. "Maybe we should. Maybe it's like that movie. I'm doomed to repeat the same clumsy mistakes over and over, every time we meet."

"Well, I made sure to dress in brown," he said, indicating his brown wool trousers and sweater. "So fire away. I'm ready."

When the table was finally cleaned up, they both sat down. The blush still stained Nina's cheeks and Cameron still wasn't sure what to say. He'd have been completely satisfied just to sit across from her and look at her pretty face, but he guessed that she expected a little more. "Is this work?" he asked, pointing to the coffee-stained papers.

Nina nodded. "It was. I've got a special project I've been assigned. I've been working on it all day."

"And where do you work?" he asked, already knowing the answer. He felt guilty even bringing up the subject of her job, considering his position, but it was a safe subject for two people who barely knew each other.

"I'm the head of research for *Attitudes,*" she said. "It's a weekly magazine. Our offices are right across the street."

He couldn't help but smile at the embellished job title. Still, he was secretly pleased that she was trying to impress him. "*Attitudes?*"

"Have you ever heard of it?" She forced a smile. "I suppose not. I mean, you're not really our type—our reader—I mean, our demographic."

"And why is that?" Cameron asked.

"Well, you're a little too..."

He waited as she groped for a polite way to say conservative. "Tall?" he asked. Her blush deepened and she shook her head. "Too stubborn? That's always been a problem." She shook her head again. "Or maybe I'm too clumsy?"

Nina laughed. "The word we'd use around the office might be 'conservative.' Not that that's a bad thing. It's just not our demographic."

"Gee, I thought you were about to say I was too handsome or too charming."

"Maybe I should have," she murmured, sending

him a coy look over the rim of her coffee mug. "So, what do you do?"

"I'm in...computers," Cameron said.

"I could have guessed that," Nina commented. "I mean, from the way you were dressed when we first met. You looked like a businessman."

A long silence grew between them and Cameron fought the sudden urge to lean across the table and kiss her, simply to see if her lips tasted as good as they looked. Instead, he grabbed the next handiest subject. "Tell me about this project you're working on." Cameron pointed to the papers. "You said it was important?" He picked up his mug and took a sip of his coffee.

"There's not much to it," Nina replied. "I'm supposed to find out everything I can about some guy named Cameron Ryder."

A sudden cough burst from his throat and he sucked in a deep breath, the coffee going down the wrong way. Nina's brow furrowed in concern and she reached out and patted him on the shoulder. "Are you all right?"

He nodded. "It's just a little hot," he said, his eyes watering. "So, what have you found out about this guy?"

"I spent all day on the Net, downloading what I could about his company, NightRyder. But the guy who runs it keeps a pretty low profile. If I had to guess I'd say he's some hard-hearted, ruthless businessman who buys up companies for sport, putting good people out of work, and he keeps a low profile so none of the

employees he puts out of work can run over him with
a bus."

"He sounds like a real bastard," Cameron said.

"This NightRyder, it's a news and information site.
Very trendy, very popular with our magazine's demographic. He wants to buy *Attitudes* and turn himself
into some media mogul. My boss doesn't want to sell."

"And what else have you learned?"

"Not much. I can't even find a photo of the guy, except for this." She slid a paper over towards him. "It's
his high school graduation picture. He looks like kind
of a geek. But I guess even geeks can turn into bastards
given enough power and money."

Cameron winced inwardly. Damn, he hated when
that picture surfaced in the media. He'd done his best
to stay out of the glare of the paparazzi, avoiding photographers like the plague. But for lack of a more current photo, they always trotted out the senior picture—
the pimply-faced, pencil-necked doofus with the thick
glasses. And he was once again faced with a reminder
of the first eighteen years of his life.

But there was one advantage to the photo. There was
no way Nina Forrester would recognize him. Hell, he
barely recognized himself. "He doesn't look very ruthless to me. He looks like the kind of kid who eats paste
and spends most of his day stuffed in a locker. See
there," he said, pointing to the picture. "He's got lou-
ver marks on his forehead."

She snatched the picture away from him and put it
back in her folder. "If he buys the magazine, I'll probably be out of a job." Nina shook her head. "But I really
don't want to think about that now." The gloomy look

dissolved from her face and she smiled again. "Why don't we talk about something else? You know, I don't even know your name."

Cameron opened his mouth, about to introduce himself, then thought better of it. She already believed him to be a ruthless bastard. If he told her who he really was she might just heave the rest of her coffee in his face. "And I don't know your name," he said, surprised with his smooth reply.

"It's Nina. Nina Forrester."

She held out her hand and he took it, grasping her delicate fingers with his. A current of electricity shot through his arm, warming his blood. How could a simple touch affect him so strongly? He wanted to lace his fingers with hers and bring them to his lips. He noticed that she was wearing green nail polish to match the deep green of her satin jacket. He liked it, even though it was an odd color. Odd looked good on her. When he felt her gently tug her fingers away, he let go.

"What about you?" she asked after a long silence.

"Me? I don't usually wear nail polish."

Nina giggled and gave him an odd look. "What's your name?"

"Oh, it's...Wright," he said, taking the first name that came to mind while still completely captivated by her eyes. After all, that's who she was looking for, wasn't it?

"Right?" she asked. "Like Mr. Right? R-I-G-H-T?"

He shook his head. "W-R- Like Wilbur and Orville. I think we might even be related."

Her brow arched. "And do you have a first name? Or would you prefer I call you Mister?"

"Jack. Jack Wright."

"It's nice to finally meet you, Jack Wright."

Suddenly, he didn't want to talk about her work. He wanted to find out much more about this enchanting woman sitting in front of him. He wanted to listen to her voice and watch the lively play of emotion on her face as she spoke. He wanted to lose himself in her brilliant blue eyes and warm himself beneath her smile. "Would you like to get out of here? Maybe take a walk or get something to eat?"

She smiled and he was certain she was about to accept his invitation, but then she shook her head. "I can't. I have a lot of work to do. My boss expects a report first thing tomorrow morning on this Cameron Ryder and I haven't found anything to give her. I'm going to have to go back to the office."

Cameron was tempted to give her everything she wanted just to spend a little more time with her. He'd tell her about his childhood, his stumbles toward puberty, the awful teenage years and the grind through college. He'd give her his banker's number, his attorney's number. Anything she wanted to know, he'd tell her. But Cameron knew that wasn't possible. For now, he was better off hiding behind the guise of Mr. Wright. "If you can't have dinner tonight, how about lunch tomorrow?"

She stood and gathered up her papers. "All right. Lunch would be fine."

Cameron slipped out of his chair and helped her into her coat, allowing his hands to rest on her shoulders for a few minutes. He leaned closer and drew a deep breath. Her hair smelled like fresh air and flowers.

Then she stepped away, walking toward the door. Cam tossed a few bills on the table for a tip, then followed her.

When they reached the sidewalk, an uneasy silence settled between them. This was the time he was supposed to say something incredibly clever or smooth, so she'd invite him back to her apartment. But Cam couldn't come up with anything except, "Can I give you a ride? We can share a cab."

Nina giggled. "I'm just going across the street."

Cameron groaned inwardly. The doofus gene had asserted itself again, just when he thought he'd managed to knock it out of his DNA. "Right," he said. He rubbed his hands together. "So, I'll see you tomorrow for lunch?"

"Lunch," she repeated. "Where?"

"I'll pick you up at your office."

She nodded, then took a step toward the curb. As she did, Nina turned back to look at him and all Cam knew at that moment was he didn't want to let her go, not yet. He grabbed her hand and pulled her closer. And then, without even considering the consequences, he brought his mouth down on hers in a soft, but hungry kiss.

Never in his life had he acted so impulsively. But with Nina, it didn't pay to think. The moments flew past so quickly, that he couldn't help but reach out and catch one and hold onto it for a time. He'd meant only to indulge in a brief kiss, but when she wrapped her arms around his neck, he gently pushed her back until she stood against the brick facade of the coffee shop.

Slowly, Cameron explored her mouth, tasting and testing. When he finally found the strength to pull away, he brought his hand up to her cheek and skimmed her silken skin.

She swallowed hard, her eyes wide and dewy. "If—if I tell you something, will you promise not to take it the wrong way?"

Cameron nodded. "I'll try."

"I was hoping you'd stop by the coffee shop tonight," she murmured. "That's why I came." A pretty blush stained her cheeks and her gaze dropped to his chest.

"And I was hoping you'd be here." He reached down and caught a finger under her chin. Then, without a second thought, he leaned forward and brushed another kiss across her lips. "I'll call you," he murmured, his eyes fixed on her mouth for a long moment.

"You don't have my phone number."

"But I know where you work," he countered. "We can decide where we want to go for lunch."

Nina nodded. "That would be nice." Slowly, reluctantly, she stepped out of his embrace. She sent him one last smile, then turned and hurried across the street. Cameron watched until she disappeared through the front door of *Attitudes*, then he let out a tightly held breath.

With a soft curse, he raked his hand through his hair and shook his head. "I sure hope you figure out what the hell you're doing, Ryder. Because once she finds out who you really are, she's not going to want to kiss you anymore. Hell, you'll be lucky if she lets you live."

"WHERE HAVE YOU BEEN? I've been waiting for you all morning!" Nina called.

Lizbeth hurried through the hallway to the fashion offices, Nina falling into step beside her. "I had a photo shoot," Lizbeth explained. "I'm just back for a few minutes. Hervé insists that we use that silly fedora. He thinks it's sexy—I just think it looks stupid."

"But I have to talk to you. Can't you stay for a few minutes?"

When they reached Lizbeth's office, Nina followed her inside and slammed the door behind her. Unlike her own office, which was neatly filled with books and binders full of useful information, Lizbeth's office looked like a bomb had exploded in a designer showroom. Clothes and accessories were scattered everywhere, hanging from shelves, tossed over chairs, folded on the floor. Nina wasn't sure how Lizbeth kept anything straight since all the clothes seemed to be black.

"I've got three minutes," Lizbeth said. "Talk fast."

"All right, here's the condensed version. I saw him again last night. We kissed, three or four times, I can't even remember. And it was so incredible. And he's coming here to take me out to lunch."

Lizbeth looked up. "What?"

"The coffee guy," Nina explained, "from Jitterbug's. His name is Wright. Can you believe that? Is that too perfect? Jack Wright. W-R, not with just an R. He was in there last night and we—"

Lizbeth held out her hand to stop Nina's words, then slowly circled her desk and sat down. "Honey, Hervé can do without that hat. Tell me all the details."

"But I thought you—"

"I have all the time in the world for your love life," Lizbeth cried.

Nina sighed, then sat down across the desk from her and began to recount the events of the night before. She made a special point of telling Lizbeth how she refused his invitation to dinner. "That was good, right? I mean, I didn't want to seem too enthusiastic, or too easy."

"You did very well."

She smiled proudly. "I did. And oh, he just makes me feel so good. I get all warm inside and my knees go a little soft and my brain doesn't seem to work right, and—and I can barely breathe. Do you know that feeling?"

Lizbeth raised an eyebrow. "Honey, I invented that feeling. Now, when is he coming to take you to lunch?"

"In about fifteen minutes," Nina said.

She gave Nina the once-over. "That gives us just enough time."

"For what?"

"To fix you up."

Nina glanced down at the outfit she'd so carefully chosen that morning. The little sweater dress was from the sixties, pale melon pink with bugle bead starbursts on the cuffs, collar and hem. She considered it a conservative choice paired with knee-high black boots. Nina had taken special care with her hair, wearing it loose and unbound in soft waves, pushed away from her face by a black headband. "What's wrong?"

"He was wearing a handmade French shirt and a designer suit, Hugo Boss if I'm not mistaken. The guy knows fashion." Lizbeth jumped to her feet and began snatching clothes from around the room—a long, pencil-thin skirt, a body-hugging sweater, both in black. "The boots are good, the rest has to go."

"Why?"

"Honey, you've got that whole groovy sixties thing going. Or maybe it's seventies, I'm not sure. If he dressed in Nehru jackets or leisure suits, then I'd say go for it but we're not playing Austin Powers today."

Nina reluctantly changed into the clothes Lizbeth had chosen, secretly pleased that she was able to fit into the sample sizes. Though the calf-length skirt nearly reached her ankles, Lizbeth pronounced that length equally fashionable. When she was dressed, her friend pulled her hair back into a sleek ponytail and tied it with an expensive black silk scarf.

Nina stood in front of the mirror that Lizbeth had cleared and looked at herself. The clothes did show her figure to its best advantage. And the black made her look even thinner and more sophisticated. But the outfit didn't have any character or color. It said nothing about the person she was. "Now I look like everyone else that lives in this city. This is like the uniform for young, professional women."

"Which is exactly what he'll like." Lizbeth's phone rang and she picked it up, then smiled at Nina. "Yup, she's here, and she'll be right out." She put the phone down. "He's in reception. Would you like me to walk out with you? Never mind, I'm going to walk out with you. But I won't act like I'm going down to see him, I'll just run across the street and get a cup of coffee."

They both headed for the reception area on the ground floor of the building. When they stepped out of the elevator, Nina saw him, sitting in an overstuffed leather chair near the window. He was focussed on the most recent issue of *Attitudes*, his brow furrowed, his expression dubious. Instead of a suit, he was wearing faded jeans that hugged his long legs and a canvas jacket that hid a T-shirt. "See," Nina said. "He's not wearing a suit."

"Yum," Lizbeth breathed. "What a hottie!" She turned and straightened Nina's collar. "Ride 'em, cow-girl."

Her friend kept walking, right out the door, and Nina stopped in front of Jack. "Hi," she said, unable to stop a smile from curling the corners of her lips.

He looked up. Surprise colored his expression as he rose to his feet, taking in her appearance. He reached out and took her hand, a gesture that seemed so natural but sent her heart racing. And when he bent and brushed a kiss on her cheek, she truly thought she might swoon. "Hi. For a minute there I didn't recognize you." His gaze slowly raked her body. "You look a little different."

"It's the clothes," Nina replied. "My friend Lizbeth lent them to me. She works in the fashion department."

"They're very...black."

"I know. I usually like more colorful things. Clothes that have more character. She's always trying to change me, trying to improve my fashion sense."

He shrugged. "I like your other clothes. They suit you."

"I could change back," Nina suggested.

Jack shook his head. "Naw. Just take that scarf out of your hair."

The scarf became history and Nina shook out her hair, then smiled. "Would you like to see my office?" she asked.

For a moment, she thought he might refuse the offer, but then he nodded. They walked back toward the elevator, his fingers woven through hers, the contact unbreakable. Even when they stepped off on the third floor, home to editorial, he refused to let go. Jack stopped short and stared at the roomful of cubicles, each one decorated in a colorful, almost outrageous manner.

Nina had never taken the time to look at it through a stranger's eyes, but it was a bit bizarre. A huge blow-up alligator hung from the ceiling along with a string of Japanese lanterns and a blinking neon sign that said Eat at Joe's. Various other silly toys and crazy posters lined the walls, giving the entire office the look of a playground for grown-ups.

"It's kind of overwhelming," he said.

"Charlotte likes to hire people who think in circular patterns rather than linearly," Nina explained. At his curious look, she laughed. "Her words. That means she likes to hire people who are really creative and... and a bit crazy and don't argue with her when she's wrong."

"She sounds like quite a boss."

Nina shrugged. "She's not so bad. I just wish she could remember my name."

"Nina," he said. She loved the way her name sounded on his lips. "How could she ever forget your name?"

Nina led him towards her office. He followed her inside then shut the door behind him. In one smooth movement, he spun her around and pulled her into his arms. His mouth came down on hers and he kissed her, softly at first and then with growing urgency. "I've been thinking about this all morning," he murmured against her mouth.

Her hands skimmed over his chest, warm and hard beneath his T-shirt. When it came to Jack Wright, she lost all resistance. "Umm," she said between kisses. "Me, too."

"Maybe we shouldn't do this," Jack said. "It's not..."

"Professional?" Nina asked. She moaned softly, then pulled away. With a wicked grin, she stepped back to her desk and, one by one, shoved books and files off until the surface was nearly bare. Then she grabbed him by the collar of his jacket and pushed him backwards.

As he hitched his hip up on the desk, he chuckled softly. "I'm pretty sure this isn't in the employee manual either."

Nina wasn't sure where she left the last traces of her inhibitions, but she really didn't care. She should be playing a little harder to get, but what harm was there in kissing? As long as it didn't go any further, then why should she worry? Besides, she liked kissing Jack Wright. It was better than eating chocolate.

She stepped between his legs and wrapped her arms around his neck. What was it about this man that made it impossible to resist him? Maybe it was his smile, that boyish grin that set her pulse racing. Or maybe it was the little streak of the conservative she caught in his nature. Or the enjoyment he seemed to find in touching and kissing her.

"Kristine!"

The door to Nina's office swung open just as she and Jack were involved in a particularly passionate kiss. With a tiny cry of alarm, Nina jumped back to find Charlotte standing in the doorway of her office. Nervously, she wiped at her damp lips, then clutched her hands in front of her.

Charlotte gave Jack a cursory glance, then turned back to Nina. "I've been waiting for your report on Ryder," she said. "Where is it?"

Nina swallowed hard, then stepped around Jack and searched the floor. "It's—it's right here. I wasn't able to find much but—"

"Do you realize how important this is, Kristine? The future of *Attitudes* is resting with you."

"Her name is Nina," Jack said, his tone barely hiding his annoyance. Nina wasn't sure whether he was upset about the intrusion or about Charlotte's inability to remember her name, but either way, the look Charlotte sent him was sharp enough to cut diamonds.

Nina's gaze jumped back and forth between the two as she crawled around on the floor, picking through papers and books. Finally, she caught sight of her report up on the desk, beneath Jack's backside. She grabbed the corner and gave it a tug. "Move," she murmured. He complied, leaning to one side until she could extract the report.

She scrambled to her feet and handed it to Charlotte. "If you'd like, we can go over it. I didn't find much, but there are some promising leads and there is some interesting financial information.''

"I'm free now," Charlotte said, her brow arched coolly.

With that, she turned and walked out of the office, leaving Nina to her own mortification. She felt Jack's arms slip around her waist. "Are you in trouble?" he asked.

She turned in his arms, then shook her head. "Probably not. You wouldn't believe some of the things that go on in this office. Good grief, the fashion department is like Sodom and Gomorrah. And those guys down in Movies and Music are completely out of control. As for Charlotte, she's not exactly the Singing Nun. No, the kiss isn't the problem. But that report is." Nina drew a shaky breath. "I really should meet with her. Can I have a rain check on lunch?"

Jack stared down into her eyes, then nodded. His fingers found her mouth and he slowly ran his thumb across her lower lip, a move that sent shivers coursing through her body. "All right," he said. "But how about this weekend? I'll pick you up tomorrow morning and we'll take off, just the two of us. No phones, no work, no interruptions."

She should have refused. Kissing Jack Wright was one thing, but going away for the weekend with a virtual stranger was another. "I—I'm not sure—"

"Separate rooms," he said. "And no expectations. We'll just have fun."

"Really?" A tiny smile curved the corners of her mouth. "All right. Yes. I think a weekend away would be wonderful." Nina reached around him and grabbed a scrap of paper from her desk, then scribbled her home phone number and address on it. She placed it in his hand. "I'll see you tomorrow."

"Tomorrow." He pushed to his feet and walked to the door, then looked back. "She really doesn't remember your name, does she?"

Nina shrugged. "She's got a lot on her mind."

Jack frowned, then nodded. "I'll pick you up at ten. Bring along warm clothes."

When she was finally alone, Nina sighed softly and smiled. A weekend away with the incredibly sexy Jack Wright. Where would they go? And what would happen? Would a few kisses lead to something much more? Another shiver skittered through her body. Was it possible that Jack would be Mr. Right *and* Mr. Right Now at the same time?

"It's going to be fun finding out," Nina said as she headed to the door.

3

"SIGN HERE AND HERE."

Cameron stared at the contract, skimming the text, yet not comprehending a single word. Though he had at least three days' work backed up at the office, he'd decided to leave it all behind and take off for the weekend with Nina. His thoughts were already on her, not on business. "I trust I'm not signing away my share in NightRyder?" he asked Jeff Myers.

They sat in the back seat of a limo, headed from the New Jersey office of NightRyder to Nina's East Village apartment. Jeff had jumped in at the last moment, hoping to convince Cam to take along a prospectus for a small Internet company he'd recommended for acquisition, but Cameron had tossed the paperwork back at him.

"Where are you going?" Jeff asked, pulling out another sheaf of papers for Cam's signature.

"You think I'd tell you?"

"I just don't think it's responsible business practice to leave town without leaving word where you're going to be. What if there's an emergency? At least take your cell phone. Or here, take my beeper."

"You can handle any problems that come up," Cameron said, leaning back into the soft leather seat. "That's what I pay you for." He stared out the window, watching the lights of the Holland Tunnel race by, an image of Nina dancing in his mind.

"You must really like this girl. I've never seen you quite so preoccupied with a woman."

Cameron shot Jeff a sideways glance. "Yeah, I like her." He frowned. "Like" didn't seem quite sufficient to describe his feelings for Nina Forrester. He was intrigued, captivated. Infatuated. "She's...different."

"How so?"

Cameron considered his answer for a long time, then sighed. "With the others, I didn't have to do anything. I mean, I'm not the most suave guy on the planet but that didn't seem to matter. I guess the money was the big drawing card. They didn't really care about the man. Hell, they were all beautiful, but there wasn't a...spark. And I really didn't care that there wasn't."

"But with this girl you do?"

"I want to make this a romantic weekend, really make an impression." He twisted to face Jeff. "You're married. What did you do to get your wife to fall in love with you?"

"What makes you think I had to *do* anything?"

"Come on, Myers. On the suave scale, you're hanging down there at the bottom with me, buddy. We share a common history. We were both computer geeks. While other guys were necking in the back seats of cars, you and I were coding HTML and taking apart modems."

Jeff chuckled. "We were both *struggling* computer geeks. Then we sold stock in our company in the midst of the technology boom. And now we're very wealthy computer geeks. That's the difference."

"I'm serious," Cam said, shifting in his seat. "I need some advice. I rented every room in the inn just so we'd be alone. And I called the innkeeper and had him put lots of fresh flowers in her room. And he's going to build a big fire for our arrival."

"What about wine? Or champagne?"

Cameron cursed beneath his breath and winced. "Champagne. Right. I missed that one." He grabbed the car phone and punched in a number he'd memorized over the past twenty-four hours. When the innkeeper picked up, Cameron greeted him apologetically. "Sorry to bother you again, Mr. Sawyer, but could you have some champagne chilling for our arrival? The very best you have." He held his hand over the receiver and looked to Jeff. "Anything else?"

"A romantic dinner? Soft music? Candlelight?"

Cam cursed again. "Hell, I *am* bad at this," he muttered. He relayed the additional orders to the innkeeper, knowing that the man would do whatever was necessary to provide for Cam's requests. After all, money had convinced the innkeeper to open early for the season, more money could buy a more romantic atmosphere.

Cameron's stomach had been in knots since he'd gotten up that morning. He'd promised Nina a wonderful time, but he wasn't all that sure he could deliver. Second doubts about a weekend together had plagued his mind. Maybe he was moving too fast, risking too much by taking her away. Maybe, given time alone with him, she'd realize what a dope he could be.

At least they'd have separate rooms. He wasn't so

presumptuous as to believe they'd share a bed so early in their relationship. That said something about him, didn't it? Cam groaned softly. Maybe it said he wasn't as smooth as he pretended to be. Any other guy would have tossed aside his doubts and seduced Nina at the very first opportunity.

"If you've really got seduction on your mind, you ought to try some of those aphrodisiac foods." Jeff reached in his briefcase and pulled out the latest issue of *Attitudes*. "I've been reading this magazine and you won't believe the stuff they print! It's all here in this article. Oysters, truffles, avocados, chocolate. They're all supposed to kick start the libido."

Cam grabbed the magazine and scanned the article. Charlotte Danforth did have a way of choosing editorial material that was both audacious and interesting at the same time. If she hadn't made such a bad impression on him in Nina's office, he might have considered keeping her on. But after seeing the hurt in Nina's eyes when her boss couldn't even remember her name, Cameron was determined that she'd be the first one out the door once he took over.

"My libido is just fine," Cam said. In truth, he wondered whether he'd be able to keep his hands off Nina. She was just so touchable, the kind of woman made for a man's hands—and a man's bed. A smile curled the corners of his mouth. *His* hands and *his* bed.

The limo wove through the narrow streets of the East Village and when they'd nearly reached Nina's apartment, Cameron leaned forward and rapped on the privacy screen. The driver immediately lowered the screen and looked at Cam in the rearview mirror. "Pull over on the next block," he ordered.

The driver did as ordered, then hopped out and circled the car to open the door on Jeff's side. Jeff frowned at Cameron. "Go on," Cam said. "Get out."

"Why?"

"Geez, Myers, I don't want *you* in the car when I pick her up," Cam replied. "That wouldn't be very romantic. Even I know that."

"But how am I supposed to get back to the office?"

"Take a cab. You can charge it to the company."

Jeff grumbled as he climbed out of the car. "Are you sure you can't leave a number so that—"

Cam reached over and pulled the door shut, then chuckled to himself. He hadn't spent a weekend away from the office in nearly a year. He deserved a break. And who better to share his first free weekend with than Nina Forrester?

His mind wandered back to their last encounter, in her office, on her desk. He wasn't sure what had gotten into them, why they'd tossed aside hesitancy and inhibition without a second thought. When it came to kissing Nina, he certainly couldn't summon much common sense. When they weren't locked in a passionate embrace he was thinking about kissing her. Maybe it was that mouth, so full and soft, so tempting. Or that body, delicate, pliable, perfect beneath his palms. Or the look in her eyes, a mix of nervous apprehension and barely concealed desire.

There would be more kisses this weekend. He'd make sure of that. But this time there'd be no one to interrupt, no clock to watch or job to run to, no boss to appease. Nothing but long endless hours looking into her eyes, watching her move, listening to her voice. And if she was willing, they would have time for more—time for slow seduction and time to test the limits of her desire.

When the limo pulled to a stop again, he glanced out the tinted window and saw Nina sitting on the front steps of her apartment building, her overnight bag at her side. She looked at the car suspiciously, her hand shielding her eyes from the sun, not quite ready to believe that this was her ride. Cam slid over and opened the door, then stepped out.

When she saw him, she smiled and waved, her blue eyes lighting up. Suddenly he was glad he'd made that second call to the innkeeper. He wanted that pretty smile to stay on her face all weekend long. He crossed the sidewalk, then reached down to take her bag from her hand. "All set?" he asked.

Nina nodded. "It was a little hard deciding what to pack since I didn't know where we were going."

Cam shrugged, then smiled. "Don't worry. If you need anything, we'll buy it."

"I've never ridden in a limo before," Nina said, as she stepped inside and settled herself on the seat. "Charlotte's always riding around town in them, but I take the bus or the subway."

Cam slid in beside her, rather than across from her. She glanced around at her surroundings and ran her hands over the leather seat. Cam couldn't help but wish she'd reach out and touch him in the same enticing way, or at least give him a sign that she might want to be kissed. "This is bigger than my bedroom," she murmured. "If it came with a bathroom, I'd move in and sublet my apartment." She smiled at him. "So are we going to spend our weekend in the back of this limo?"

He sent her a wicked grin. "I think you'll find my plans much more exciting than the back seat of a limo."

They sat silently as the limo pulled away from the curb, sending each other furtive smiles as Cam scrambled for something to talk about. This was the problem, he mused. He'd just never perfected the fine art of small talk and if there was anything a woman liked it was small talk. One moment, he could be on a roll, charming, polished, even witty. And the very next minute, he could barely put together a coherent sentence.

"Maybe we should just get it over with," Nina murmured, staring down at her fingers.

"What is that?" he asked.

"You know...the kiss. I mean, after what happened in my office, it's not like we've never kissed before. And rather than think about it all the way to wherever we're going, we could just...do it."

"We could," Cam said softly. He reached up and stroked his finger along her jawline. "Or we could wait."

Nina swallowed hard. "Maybe that would be best," she replied.

They stared at each other for a long time, neither one making a move. Cam knew he wanted to kiss her and from the look in her eyes, she wasn't about to refuse him. He'd been thinking about nothing else since the last time they'd seen each other. But he wasn't quite sure what she wanted. A simple kiss, a brush of their lips? Or something more passionate, something deeper and more stirring? After what had happened on her desk, there was no telling what might go on in the privacy of the limo's back seat.

In her office, he had operated on instinct alone, but now that he had time to think about it, perhaps he should take a more measured approach. No, he wouldn't kiss her. Not until everything had been cleared up between them. This weekend, he was determined to tell Nina exactly who he was. He'd already gone way too far in his deception. In truth, he'd never intended to go beyond that second night in the coffee shop. But then, he'd kissed her and all his good intentions had been lost.

Once he told her the truth, everything would be so much easier between them. He'd take her face in his hands, capture her mouth with his, and they'd start all over. And she'd know she wasn't kissing some guy named Jack. She'd be kissing Cameron Ryder and she'd be enjoying it.

He reached over and took her hand, lacing his fingers through hers. "I have an idea," he murmured, gently stroking the back of her hand with his thumb. "Why don't we just wait and see what develops along the way? After all, we have the whole weekend ahead of us."

NINA SANK into the steaming hot water in the antique tub. The bath warmed the chill right out of her bones, slowing her pulse, bringing a sheen of perspiration to her skin and allowing her to drift into an easy lethargy.

They'd arrived at the inn on the coast of Maine shortly after noon, their chartered plane landing at a small airport in a nearby town. Separate rooms had been prepared for them on the quiet second floor, their doors across the hall from each other at the end of the hallway. Nina's room was spacious and filled with antiques. A fireplace crackled cheerfully on her arrival and vases filled with fresh flowers greeted her.

They had dropped their bags, put on a few layers of sweaters, then headed out to explore the area. Still too early for the tourist season, the streets of the picturesque oceanside village were nearly as empty as the inn. And as she and Jack shared the afternoon, they'd grown even closer, relating details of their lives, laughing and teasing, as if they'd known each other for years. After lunch, they'd explored the bluffs above the town, the sea wind bringing a healthy color to her cheeks and the tang of salt sharpening her senses. By the time they'd finally come in, she was cold to the core.

Cold or warm, she'd never spent a more exhilarating afternoon. They ate lunch at a restaurant overlooking the harbor, a hearty clam chowder and crusty bread. And later, he bought her a little seagull carved out of wood by a local artisan and she bought him a cap with the front half of a lobster sticking out of the crown. She'd commented on the extravagance of the weekend, determined to find a way to thank him, but he'd brushed it off, saying simply that the computer business paid very well.

They stayed out until the sun dipped toward the horizon, then hiked back up to the inn set on a bluff above the Atlantic. There was only one low point to the day. Though he'd held her hand and touched her without hesitation, even nuzzled her neck playfully, Jack hadn't kissed her all day long. Nina was beginning to regret her request to get it out of the way, wondering if maybe she'd spoiled the entire weekend with her impulsive request in the car.

She tipped her head back and brushed a damp tendril from her face. The day wasn't over yet. Downstairs, the innkeeper was setting a table in front of the huge fireplace where she and Jack would share an intimate supper. For now, Nina would simply have to savor the anticipation of what the night might bring. She stretched out her leg and rested it on the old-fashioned faucet, examining the curve of her calf and wondering if Jack found her legs attractive.

Idly, she drew her toe around and around the tub's faucet, caught in a delicious memory from that afternoon. She could still feel his arms warm around her waist, his chest hard against her back as they stood overlooking the Atlantic. What strange bit of luck had brought him into her life? A cup of coffee purchased at just the right moment in just the right place? Or was it something more?

Though she'd dated all sorts of men, she'd never met a man quite like Jack. He had a subtle confidence about him, quiet and intense, a strength underlying his every action and word. Maybe that was it—Jack Wright wasn't a boy trying to act like a man. He was a man, a handsome and desirable man, a man she couldn't stop herself from wanting.

A tremor raced through her body, settling in her

stomach. What would the next hours bring? He'd have to kiss her good-night. It was expected, wasn't it? But after that, she wasn't sure where she wanted the night to lead. Though she'd never gone to bed with a man on the first date, she'd already decided that this technically wasn't a first date. They'd met that night in the coffee shop so the first date would have been the next night. The second date could have been the kiss they'd shared in her office. So technically, this was the third date and the third date rule was quite common.

Besides, she didn't need rules to tell her how she felt about Jack. Or how he felt about her. She could see it in his eyes every time he looked at her. Nina sighed. But was she simply trying to rationalize a healthy case of lust? Sure, they'd grown close and their desire for each other sometimes overwhelmed common sense, but they were still nearly strangers.

Who was this man who had swept her away with his sexy smiles and his boyish charm? At first glance, he appeared to be just one of the many successful businessmen who wandered the streets of Manhattan, perfectly dressed, focussed, confident. The kind of man that always had a beautiful woman walking beside him. But beneath the surface there was an odd detachment, a vulnerability that she caught every now and then in his words. There were moments that afternoon, when she'd looked up at him and found him captivated by some silly remark she'd made, then wondered why he found her so interesting.

"Why am I here?" she murmured, sinking deeper into the tub. "I'm not exactly the kind of girl a guy like Jack probably dates."

And he certainly wasn't her typical boyfriend. She'd always gravitated toward more creative types—struggling artists, penniless musicians, actors working as waiters. A big night out was a movie and half a corned beef sandwich at the Stage Deli. Nothing close to a weekend in Maine, complete with limo, private plane, gourmet food and fancy wine.

A drip of cold water plunked into the bathtub at her feet and she distractedly stuck her big toe against the end of the faucet. "Why am I here?" she repeated, twisting her toe into the spout and pulling it out again, the repetitive action distracting her mind. "What does he want from me?"

Her thoughts focussed on the questions plaguing her mind as she pushed her toe further into the spout. But this time, it didn't come back out again. Nina frowned, then levered up out of the water. She gave her foot a sharp tug. Like a Chinese finger puzzle, the harder she pulled, the tighter the spout held onto her big toe. A knock sounded on her room door and Nina grabbed her foot and pulled.

"Miss Forrester?" The voice of the innkeeper echoed through from the hallway into the tiled bathroom, the nearly closed bathroom door muffling the sound slightly. "Miss Forrester?"

"Yes?" Nina called.

"Dinner will be served in another thirty minutes. Mr. Wright is waiting for you to join him downstairs whenever you're ready."

"Thank you!" Nina called. She grabbed a bar of soap and frantically scrubbed at her toe, trying to push some of the lather up the spout. But it seemed the more she worked at freeing herself, the more painful and swollen her toe became.

"This is ridiculous. Just grit your teeth and pull it out!" Nina took a deep breath, preparing herself for the pain. But it was too much to bear and she quit pulling when it felt like her toe was about to rip off her foot. She glanced around the bathroom, hoping that she might find a spare pipe wrench lying around. But this bathroom only offered incredibly soft towels and antique accessories, and a pretty little African violet on the windowsill. There wasn't even a phone for her to call for help!

Nina moaned softly. "They're going to find me tomorrow morning, all shriveled up and naked." She continued to twist and turn and frantically search for a way to regain possession of her toe and escape her embarrassing predicament. She wasn't sure how much time had passed, but when the water began to turn cold, she reached for the faucet, hoping that the pressure of turning it on might force her toe out. But it didn't work.

The next fifteen minutes passed slowly as Nina tried to figure out a way to summon a plumber without Jack knowing about it. Then, another knock sounded at the door and a sigh of relief slipped from her lips. The innkeeper would know what to do and she was sure she could swear him to silence to avoid any further embarrassment. "Come in," she called. "The door's unlocked." The latch clicked and the hinges creaked. "Can you wait out there?"

"Nina? What's going on? Dinner is ready."

Her eyes went wide and her heart sank. Jack! Oh, no,

why had she invited *him* in? If he wandered into the bathroom, she'd be completely humiliated, stark naked, shivering, her toe shoved into the spout. "I'll be right down," she said. "I'm just finishing up in here." She sank down in the cold soapy water. "By the way, could you ask the innkeeper to come back up?"

"Why?"

"Nothing important. There's a—a leak. I've kind of plugged it for now but I think it might be a problem. Tell him he'll probably need a pipe wrench. The dripping was driving me a little—crazy. I don't think I'll be able to sleep with it."

She heard soft footsteps on the hardwood floors, but they weren't walking toward the door, they were coming closer to the bathroom. "If there's a problem, they can give you another room." He knocked softly on the door and it opened a few more inches.

A tiny scream slipped from Nina's throat and she reached above her head and grabbed a towel from the rack. She tossed it over her naked body. "Don't come in," she warned.

"Nina, what's wrong?" His voice was laced with concern and confusion.

"Nothing. Nothing at all."

He pushed the door open a few more inches. "Are you decent?"

She groaned and covered her flaming face with her hands. There was no way around it. She might as well show Jack what an idiot she really was and get it over with. He was bound to figure it out sooner or later. "Not really. But I guess you might as well come in."

He opened the door, but the minute he caught sight

of her, he covered his eyes. "You're still in the bath-tub."

"I'm kind of stuck here," she admitted.

Jack peeked out from under his hand. His gaze followed the length of her leg to the spot where she'd caught her big toe. He blinked in surprise. "Stuck?"

She nodded, her face the only warm part of her body. "Could you call the innkeeper?"

Without a second thought, he strode into the bathroom and bent down at the end of the tub, staring at her toe. He cradled her calf in his hand and a flood of heat raced up her limb and washed over her exposed skin. That was one way to get warm.

"What were you doing?" he asked.

"Plugging a leak." He slid his hand down to her foot. Though she felt completely humiliated, she also felt a little exposed. The wet towel didn't completely hide her naked body beneath. Instead, it clung to every curve like a second skin.

"It's probably just a matter of breaking the vacuum," he said.

"I—I'd really rather that you called the innkeeper," Nina said, crossing her arms over her breasts. "Or maybe his wife?"

"Just let me give this a try," he murmured, his entire attention focussed on her foot.

Nina grimaced. "I think I saw this on *Nick At Night*. Maybe it was *I Love Lucy*, or *That Girl*, but I'm pretty sure they had to call a plumber."

Jack glanced around the bathroom, then grabbed a Q-tip from a small jar near the sink. He pulled off the cotton, then tried to jam the stick between her toe and the faucet. But the stick only bent. He sat back on his heels. "It's really stuck. I think we'll have to call a plumber." Jack pushed to his feet. "I'll go get the inn-keeper."

Nina reached out to stop him, quickly covering her breasts with her other arm. "Before you do that, can you grab one of those robes from the armoire. I want to let the water out of the tub and put the robe on before I entertain any more guests."

He did as she asked, laying the robe over the edge of the tub. She watched his gaze skim her body, lingering for a moment on her breasts before slowly moving to her hips and her legs. She should have been humili-ated, but the look on his face, the carefully concealed need, the raw hunger, brought only a rush of desire. Even in such a ridiculous situation, he had the ability to make her feel sexy.

"Do you need me to help you with anything else?" he murmured, his eyes flickering before returning to her face.

Nina drew a shaky breath. Sure she needed help. She needed a way to go back in time, just an hour or so, just before that very stupid moment she'd stuck her toe in the fixture. But since she wasn't about to let him help her into the bathrobe, there wasn't anything Jack could do to alleviate her problem—except leave. "I'm sure I'll be fine," she said with a weak smile.

He gave her a shrug, then walked out of the bath-room, allowing her to drain the tub and wrestle her body into the damp terry cloth. "If you hadn't already proved that you're a complete nitwit," she muttered, "you have now." She cursed softly as she yanked on the robe. "So much for romance. He's not going to be able to look at you without bursting into gales of laughter."

BY THE TIME the plumber arrived, a small party had gathered in Nina's bathroom. The innkeeper and his wife, their handyman, the kid who delivered the produce, and the local priest. The priest had been called in case the problem turned fatal and last rites had to be performed. Apparently, there had been another death in a bathtub recently and the townsfolk were particularly sensitive to the needs of those in similar situations.

Considering the look on Nina's face, Cameron thought she just might be ready for last rites. She looked as if she might die—from embarrassment. She'd managed to wrap the robe around her naked body but from Cam's vantage point at the end of the bathtub, the gaping neckline revealed a tantalizing view of flesh. The sweet length of her thigh, the gentle curve of her neck and the intriguing cleft between her breasts.

"These antique fixtures can be a real problem," the plumber said, staring at Nina's foot as he scratched his grizzled chin. "Ah-yup. Them threads might just be seized up tight. And me without my blowtorch."

Nina's eyes went wide. "Bl—blowtorch?"

"Is that really necessary?" Cam asked. "She could be hurt."

"I 'spect that toe's throbbin' mighty bad as it is," the plumber said. "Am I right, little lady?"

Nina sent Cam a pleading look. She'd already been

stuck in the tub for nearly ninety minutes and he could
see behind the panic and humiliation and frustration.
She was close to tears.

"Would all of you excuse us for a moment?" Cam
asked. He ushered the quintet out of the bathroom,
then closed the door behind them. When he turned
back to Nina, a tear slipped from the corner of her eye.
Compassion welled up inside of him and Cam felt an
instant need to soothe her, to protect her, to rain kisses
all over her beautiful face.

But there was something else that tugged at his
heart. A deeper emotion he couldn't put into words.
What was it, this connection he felt to her? Any other
man might be angry or impatient with such silliness.
But Nina's situation—and her mortification—only
made him love her more.

The sudden realization brought him up short. Love?
How could he possibly be in love with Nina Forrester?
He barely knew her! Yet as he looked into her eyes and
watched that tear dribble down her cheek, he knew his
feelings for Nina were more intense, more soul-deep
than any he'd ever felt before. Nina was a woman he
could love and maybe he would love—for the rest of
his life. And no matter what screwy situation she got
herself into, he planned to always find a way to make
her feel better.

"Please don't look at me like that," she murmured.
"I—I know I've ruined everything. You spent all this
money on our weekend and you had a wonderful dinner planned for us and it's probably as cold and pruny
as I am right now."

Pulled from his thoughts, Cam bent down next to the

tub and took her chilly fingers in his, placing them to his lips and warming them with his breath. "Forget about the money. And dinner doesn't matter. I came here to be with you and whether that's sitting across a candlelit table or sitting on a bathroom floor, it's all the same."

"Really?" she asked, sniffling through the tears that moistened her eyes.

Cam brushed a tendril of hair from her face, then let his hand drift to the nape of her neck. He gently pulled her forward, then kissed her lips, lingering just a moment before pulling away. "Really," he assured her.

Her tears dissolved into a wide smile. "I guess we should think about getting my toe unstuck. Unless you want to spend the rest of our weekend in this bathtub with me."

The idea was certainly tempting and it caused an unbidden image to flash in Cam's mind. The two of them, naked and needy, lying in the warm water, bubbles frothing up around them. She would be nestled between his legs, her back against his chest. His hands would skim over her moist skin, exploring every curve, every sweet inch of flesh until the bath slowly became a spot for seduction. She'd turn to him, rise up above him then settle herself on top of him. And slowly, exquisitely, he'd begin to make love to her, moving inside her until she cried out—

"Maybe you should call the plumber back in here."

Cam blinked, startled out of his brief, but pleasurable daydream. "What? Oh, right." He pushed to his feet. "Yeah, I'll get the plumber. Right away."

Nina gave him an odd look, then nodded. Cam hurried from the bathroom, pushing aside the warm desire that pulsed through his bloodstream. He found the group gathered near the fireplace in Nina's room, discussing the merits of copper pipe versus lead. He cleared his throat. "You can go back in now," he said.

All five of them headed toward the bathroom door, but Cam held out his hand, letting only the plumber pass. "The rest of you can get back to whatever it was you were doing. I'm sure we can take care of this on our own."

The innkeeper gave a worried look toward the bathroom, obviously more concerned about his antique fixtures than Nina's comfort or the prognosis for saving her big toe. "Don't worry," Cam said. "Whatever the damages, I'm perfectly willing to pay." That seemed to mollify him and he, his wife, the town priest, and the produce boy hurried out.

Cam headed back toward Nina's bathroom. But the plumber emerged just as he was about to reach for the door. "She's all right now," he said. "I got her loose."

Cam reached for his wallet, then pressed a hundred dollar bill and his business card into the plumber's hand, anxious to get to Nina. "Thanks for your help," he muttered. "Just send me the bill." But when he stepped inside the bathroom, Nina was struggling to get out of the tub, the clunky spout still stuck to her foot! He gasped. "What the—?"

"My toe is swollen. The plumber says if I put some ice on it, it should pop right out. If not, I'll have to go to the hospital and they'll have to cut it off."

"Your toe?"

"No!" Nina cried. "The faucet."

In a few long steps, Cam crossed the room and helped her stand. But with the heavy metal fixture still caught on her toe, she could barely keep herself upright. He slipped his arm behind her knees and scooped her up. "Then we'll take you to the hospital," he murmured as he carried her out into the bedroom.

He set her down on the bed, nearly tumbling on top of her to maintain his balance. He froze, his hands braced on either side of her body, his face so near hers he could feel the warmth of her breath against his cheek. Cam's gaze wandered along her shoulder, to the spot where her robe had fallen away. Mesmerized by the play of light on her smooth skin, he leaned forward and dropped a kiss on that very spot.

A soft sigh slipped from Nina's lips, tickling his ear. "I—I don't want to go to the hospital," she said, her voice quiet, breathless.

Cam moved to a spot at the base of her neck and kissed her again. "Well, you can't very well live with that thing on your toe," he murmured, his lips grazing her warm skin. "You'd never be able to find shoes that fit."

A tiny shudder racked her body as Cam nuzzled his face into the curve of her shoulder, nibbling at her damp skin. "Then I'll—oh," she breathed. "I'll just have to—oh, that's nice—I'll go—I'll go—"

He pushed up and looked into her eyes. "You'll go?"

Nina swallowed hard. "Barefoot," she murmured. "I'll go barefoot."

Cam chuckled, then slowly brought his weight over her body. She sank back into the pillows, her gaze locked with his. He knew if he kissed her again, if he

took full possession of her mouth, that it would be
nearly impossible to stop there. She looked so delicious, so willing, her naked body wrapped in a robe
that could be dispatched with a few flicks of his fingers.

Reaching up, he drew his finger from her temple to
her chin. "Have I told you how beautiful you look tonight?"

"I look silly," she replied, reaching for her hair.

His finger continued a path along her jaw and down
her neck. "Your toe looks silly, but the rest of you is incredibly beautiful." To prove his point, he slipped his
hand beneath the thick terry-cloth collar and splayed
his hand over the skin just above her breast. Beneath
his palm, her heart beat a rapid rhythm. "Are you still
cold?"

Nina shook her head. Cam's gaze fixed on her
mouth, on her damp lips, full and soft, and his self control wavered. Just one more kiss and he'd leave her to
get ready for a trip to the hospital. One more taste was
all he'd need to be satisfied.

But that one taste turned into two and then three,
and before he could catch himself, he got caught in a
maelstrom of need. The need to touch her and to be
close to her, to feel her skin against his palms was overwhelming. He grabbed Nina around the waist and
rolled her on top of him, settling her along the length of
his body and raking his hands through her damp and
tangled hair.

He molded her mouth to his, probing and seeking,
the taste of her seeping into his blood like a drug. Why
had he never found this passion with any other
woman? Why Nina? The answers didn't make a

difference. All Cam knew was that this was the woman he wanted, now, always.

A soft moan slipped from her throat and she wriggled on top of him, pushing against his chest until she'd managed to sit up. Her legs bent at either side of his hips, Nina stared down at him through eyes hazy with desire, through her mussed hair. The robe gaped open until he could see the dusky tip of one of her nipples. He'd tasted her mouth and now he wanted to taste her there, to tease the soft nub with his tongue until she cried out with pleasure.

Slowly, deliberately, she pushed the robe off her shoulders, letting it fall to her waist. He saw no hesitation in her eyes, no modesty in her actions. She was as comfortable revealing her body as he was gazing upon it. Cam held his breath as he reached out to cup her breast in his hand. The soft flesh fit perfectly against his palm and when he grazed her nipple with his thumb, Nina closed her eyes and tipped her head back, revelling in the pleasure.

This was why he'd never found such passion with another woman. He was meant to be with Nina Forrester. Perhaps from the moment he was born, this moment was destined to be. Cam pushed up from the pillows and wrapped his arms around her waist. His lips found her nipple and he drew it into his mouth, provoking the very cry of pleasure he sought.

With frantic fingers, Nina began to work the buttons of his shirt open and when she couldn't work fast enough, Cam brushed her hands away and tore the shirt open himself. Her hands immediately went to his

bare chest, smoothing and skimming over every inch
of skin as if she too wanted to know him more intimately.

And then she moved back and began to fumble with
his belt. Cam groaned softly as her fingers grazed
across the hard ridge beneath his jeans. Already, he
craved her touch, the feel of her hand closing over him,
gently stroking him. "Ah, Nina," he murmured, "what
are you doing to me?"

She glanced up at him, then pushed her hair out of
her eyes. "The same thing you're doing to me."

When she'd finally freed him, the sensations of her
touch were more than he could bear. Cam reached
down and grabbed her hand to stop her and their eyes
met. "Make love to me," she said.

The request was simple and heartfelt and he could
find no hesitation behind the words. She wanted him
as much as he wanted her.

"Please, Jack," she pleaded.

A single word penetrated the haze of his desire, cutting into his brain and forcing his mind back to reality.
Jack. She'd called him Jack. That wasn't his name. But
whose name was it? In the midst of her need, had she
called out another man's name?

But as Cam focussed his thoughts on that one
word—Jack—he remembered that for all Nina knew,
that was *his* name. To her, he wasn't Cameron Ryder,
ruthless businessman and corporate raider. He was
Jack Wright, the man she'd met in a coffee shop, the
man who had whisked her away for a romantic weekend on the seacoast of Maine.

He'd fully intended to tell her the truth over dinner

and let the chips fall where they may. But then all this had happened and his good intentions had been put aside without a second thought. He couldn't go any further, not without setting her straight.

Summoning every ounce of resolve he possessed, Cam wrapped his arms around her waist and rolled to his side, setting her far enough away so that his body no longer touched hers. She closed her eyes and smiled, waiting for him to join with her, to make wild, passionate love to her. And when he didn't, she opened her eyes.

"We shouldn't do this," he said, the words sounding like they'd been uttered by a stranger.

"Why?" she asked, confusion quickly replacing desire.

"It's—it's too soon." He sat up and moved to the edge of the bed. "It's not that I don't want to make love to you, Nina. I want nothing more in this world, believe me."

"I feel the same way," she said, reaching out to touch his shoulder.

He drew a deep breath, the slowly let it out. "Then trust me on this. This isn't the right time." Cam pushed to his feet and looked back at her. The robe barely covered her body, the fabric twisted at her waist and held only by the belt. He glanced down at her foot and noticed that sometime during their encounter the antique fixture had fallen off her big toe. He smiled weakly. "I guess we don't need a trip to the hospital."

She pushed up on her elbows and held up her leg. A frown touched her lips. "I guess not," she said in a quiet voice.

"Why don't I go see about dinner while you get dressed?" He slowly walked toward the door, straightening his clothes along the way. "I'll be waiting for you downstairs."

It took all Cam's willpower to walk out of her room and shut the door behind him. His instincts told him that he may have just given up the only chance he'd ever have to make love with Nina. But it would have been won through deceit. There was no telling what the future would hold, especially after she learned he was the hated Cameron Ryder.

"We will have another chance to be together," he murmured, leaning back against the door. "I swear I'll make it happen and when it does, nothing will stop us."

4

NINA HURRIED down the sidewalk, still a block from the front door of *Attitudes*. Clouds obscured the sun, but she wore her sunglasses anyway—to hide bleary, bloodshot eyes. Sooner or later, she was going to keel over from lack of sleep. In the five nights since she met Jack, she hadn't managed more than a few hours of solid slumber. Her job worries, her embarrassment at the hands of antique plumbing products, an overwhelming desire for a man she barely knew—they'd all combined to make sleep impossible to find.

Last night had been the worst. Jack had dropped her off at her apartment on Sunday evening, brushing a chaste kiss on her cheek outside her front door. And though she'd gone to bed early, determined to catch up on lost snooze time, she spent the night tossing and turning, her body edgy with nerves and her mind caught up in endless speculation. To make matters worse, her toe still hurt.

Though she'd had a wonderful time with Jack, nothing about their weekend together made sense! Sunday had been filled with long walks and quiet talks. But considered alongside their little encounter in her four-poster bed the evening before, his circumspect behavior became fuel for endless analysis. Yet the more she tried to sort it out, the more confused she got.

Again and again, she'd replayed that single moment of passion, the instant she'd begged him to make love to her. Even now, the memory of it caused a warm flush to heat her cheeks and a soft flutter to grow in her belly. By all accounts, they'd nearly succumbed, nearly lost themselves in the ultimate intimacy—until he'd called an end to it.

Damn, she ought to be pleased! After all, there were precious few gentlemen left in the world and the last thing she wanted was a man taking advantage of her, his only thought of carving another notch into his bedpost! Nina yanked open the front door of *Attitudes*, then started across the lobby, lost in her thoughts.

But then, that wasn't her problem, was it? She wanted Jack taking every advantage. When Jack touched her and kissed her, it was more than just lusting, it was...delicious...exhilarating...and full of the promise of incredible pleasure. What girl wouldn't want that?

"I should just be happy he behaved like a gentleman," Nina murmured. "A man like that doesn't come along every day." But even that rationalization didn't diminish the tiny sliver of disappointment she felt. Was she simply not woman enough to tempt him any further? Maybe he didn't care for her body. Maybe her breasts were too small or her hips too round. Or maybe it was the awful incident in the bathtub. How could any man be sexually attracted to a woman with antique plumbing stuck to her foot?

"Nina!"

Startled out of her daydream, Nina stopped short as she reached the elevator doors, then turned back to the receptionist. She'd forgotten her usual greeting, her thoughts of Jack interfering with common courtesy. "Morning, Kathy."

"You looked like you were in another world," the receptionist said.

"Did I?"

Kathy nodded. "Hey, Charlotte is looking for you. She's been calling down here every five minutes since before eight."

"Are you sure she's looking for me?" Nina asked, impatience creeping into her tone. "She has a real problem with my—"

"Your name. I know. But since we have no Nanette, I figured she wanted you." Kathy leaned forward. "I think she slept here again last night. The business press heard about the offer from NightRyder and the buzzards are circling. Be careful," she warned. "She's in a mood."

By the time Nina got to Charlotte's office, the slightly sick feeling in her stomach that she'd attributed to missing breakfast had turned into a knot of nerves. As if her weekend with Jack wasn't enough to worry about, now she had Charlotte to contend with. Her boss was hard enough to take when Nina was prepared, but on an empty stomach and with precious little sleep, Nina felt as though she were about to jump headfirst into a snake pit.

She knocked softly, then pushed open Charlotte's office door, only to find her boss was occupied with important business. She was throwing darts at a picture taped to a dartboard, the same dartboard usually found in the entertainment editor's office. Charlotte glanced over her shoulder. "Nanette," she muttered, as she heaved another dart. "It's about time. Our workday starts at 9:00 a.m. and it's now—" She glanced at her diamond-encrusted watch. "Well, it's 9:08 a.m." This time the dart found its mark, skewering the photo in the throat.

"I'm sorry," Nina murmured. "And it's Nina, Ms. Danforth. My name is Nina Forrester, not Nanette." It was about time she stood up to her boss. This was a first step, insisting that Charlotte get her name right.

"My therapist suggested this," Charlotte explained. "It's supposed to get rid of the anger and the negative energy." The last dart found the forehead on the photo, before she turned back to Nina. "Is there something you have for me this morning?"

Nina clasped her hands in front of her. "Not really. Nothing more than I gave you Friday afternoon. I've been scouring the Internet for information on Cameron Ryder all weekend," she lied. "But I haven't found much, other than the prepackaged publicity that his own company doles out. Since their stock offering, Cameron Ryder is a multimillionaire. He retained 36 percent of NightRyder, his partner, Jeff Myers, holds 15 percent and the stockholders have the rest. Maybe we should hire a professional investigator to—"

"And where would we get the money?" Charlotte demanded. "This magazine is nearly broke."

Nina winced, her eyes darting to the expensive watch on Charlotte's wrist. If she really had the courage, she'd suggest selling it. The price alone could pay Nina's salary for the next three or four months. "I'll just have to try harder." She sighed. "I haven't even been able to find a current photo."

"Never mind the photo," Charlotte said. "I have a photo. I called a friend who does the society column for the *Post*." She pointed to the dartboard. "There he is. Mr. Cameron Ryder. Caught at a restaurant opening in TriBeCa."

Nina slowly crossed the room, squinting at the grainy photo. Something seemed familiar about the man. Though the photo was just a profile, there was a certain quality...She reached up and yanked out the dart piercing his forehead, and another piercing his cheek.

"Oh," she murmured, her heart stopping dead. "This can't be." She turned to Charlotte. "This can't be Cameron Ryder."

"Why not?"

Nina swallowed hard, forcing herself to take another breath before she looked back at the picture. It couldn't be Cameron Ryder because Cameron Ryder was a man she'd never met. And the man in the photo was most definitely a man she'd met. The man in the photo was Jack Wright.

"I thought I recognized him, too," Charlotte grumbled. "He seems...familiar. We've probably been to some of the same parties. Ships that pass in the night."

Of course he seemed familiar, Nina mused. Charlotte had seen him just a few days ago, in Nina's office, wrapped in Nina's arms! Her heart pounded and her mind whirled. What was she supposed to do now? Nina glanced around. All she wanted was the safety and solitude of her office and time to think, time to figure out what this all meant. "I—I could really use this photo," she finally said. "For my research."

"Go ahead," Charlotte said with a dramatic wave of her hand. "It's served its purpose."

Nina quickly pulled it from the dartboard, folded it in half and tucked it under her arm. "I'll just get to work. If you need me, just page me." She swallowed hard. "Nina Forrester. N-I-N-A."

She rushed out of Charlotte's office, her pulse pounding in her head, her breath coming in short gasps. When she reached a quiet corner of the hallway, she unfolded the photo and stared at it. She was right. The man in the photo was definitely Jack Wright. It was all there—the chiseled jaw, the strong mouth, the expressive gaze.

She tried to put it all together, bringing order to her chaotic thoughts. If his name was really Cameron Ryder, why did he tell her his name was Jack Wright? Nina ran back through her memories, then realized that she'd mentioned Cameron Ryder before he'd even introduced himself at the coffee shop. "I called him a hard-hearted, ruthless businessman. And I called him a bastard."

Nina moaned and rubbed her forehead. That might be good motivation for lying, especially if he'd found himself attracted to her. She glanced down at the photo again. But then, maybe this was just a big mistake. Maybe the man in the photo wasn't Cameron Ryder, or Jack Wright, or—

"I have to talk to Lizbeth," Nina murmured. "She'll know what to do."

When she got to her friend's office, she hurried inside and slammed the door behind her. Lizbeth was standing behind her desk, pensively staring at a pair of pants hung up on the edge of a picture frame.

"We need to talk," Nina said.

"Look at these," Lizbeth demanded. She pointed accusingly to the pair of cropped pants.

"Capri pants," Nina said. "Very nice. And surprise, they're black! What a novel fashion idea. We need to talk."

"Yeah, right. But they're for men. I won't name the famous designer who's pushing these, but I personally think he's been sniffing too much spray starch. These are not manly pants! Men have nice legs, but not *that* nice."

"Stop with the pants!" Nina cried. "I'm having a crisis!"

Lizbeth snatched the hanger from the frame. "And you don't think capri pants for men are a crisis? Charlotte made some silly deal with this designer and I'm supposed to show these in a June issue. I think it's time you get your priorities in order." Lizbeth turned to face her. "Well, maybe your crisis is a little worse. Honey, if those circles under your eyes get any darker we'll be calling you Zorro."

Nina held out the photo full of little dart holes. "Look at this."

Grudgingly, Lizbeth gave the photo a quick glance. "So? It's a picture of the new man in your life. Very nice."

"*This* is a picture of Cameron Ryder. The man who wants to snatch *Attitudes* out from under Charlotte

Danforth's control. The man who holds our futures in his hand."

"Don't be silly," Lizbeth said, waving her hand. "That's your friend Jack."

"My friend Jack *is* Cameron Ryder! I've been sleeping with the enemy!"

Lizbeth gasped, letting the offensive capris drop to the floor. "You slept with Jack?"

"Cameron," Nina corrected. "His name is Cameron Ryder. And, no, I haven't slept with him." She cursed softly. "Not in the technical sense. Or the Biblical sense. Although we spent some time in the same bed this weekend."

"How much time?" Lizbeth asked.

"Not enough to actually...well, there was a lot of heavy breathing and bare skin." Nina pressed her palms to her flaming face. "This is just my luck. I finally find Mr. Right and he turns out to be Mr. Could-He-Be-Any-More-Wrong?" An uneasy realization slowly seeped into her mind, a notion she didn't want to recognize. But she did anyway. "Do you think he did this all on purpose?" At Lizbeth's confused frown, she continued. "Do you think he's using me to get information about the magazine? About Charlotte?"

Lizbeth considered the notion for a long moment. "Maybe. What would you do if he was?"

Confusion quickly turned to anger as Cameron Ryder's motives became clear. Of course! He knew where she worked—why not use her for his own unscrupulous reasons? And she, the naive little dupe, had just opened the door and let him walk in. "I'd—I'd—stop seeing him! I won't let him use me. There must be a law against this. He lied to me! And then he seduced me. We'll call the SEC and file a complaint."

But though Nina knew she ought to feel a fair amount of anger and indignation, underneath it all she still wanted to believe Jack—or Cameron Ryder or whoever she'd kissed—was an honorable man. She'd seen the emotion in his eyes when he'd laid her down on the bed. Even if he was a confirmed reprobate, no man could fake it that well. He had feelings for her, she was sure of it! Besides, he'd never pushed for information about her job or her boss, not beyond what she'd offered.

Nina drew a ragged breath. "What should I do?"

Lizbeth shrugged. "Maybe you should get some motives of your own," she suggested. "He knows Charlotte is gathering information on him. But he doesn't know *you* know he knows. You use him. And in the end, you'll save the magazine and Charlotte will forever be in your debt. Honey, you could come out of this as a senior editor at *Attitudes*."

Nina shook her head. "I can't. How can I look him in the face and lie to him?"

"Honey, he's been lying to you. What's so hard? Men and women lie to each other all the time. What if you'd found out he was married? Would you be quite so righteous then?"

"Yes," Nina said firmly. "I'd do the same thing." She drew in a shaky breath, then forced the words from her mouth. "I'm going to stop seeing him. He's supposed to pick me up tonight for dinner at seven and I just won't answer the door." She pushed to her feet.

"That's exactly what I'll do. As far as I'm concerned, it's over between us. We're back to being strangers."

But once she said the words, Nina knew they weren't true. What she'd shared with Jack Wr—Cameron Ryder was special. And though he had deceived her, she had to believe he'd had his reasons. Another realization hit her like a slap on the face. Maybe he *was* married and that's why he'd lied! Nina moaned softly as her heart twisted in her chest.

"Fine," Lizbeth said. "Suit yourself. But I think you're missing a golden opportunity. Now, let's deal with my problem. Honey, what am I supposed to do with these pants?"

But Nina didn't bother to stick around to answer Lizbeth's questions. Her thoughts were on the evening ahead. She'd dumped a few guys in her life, but she'd always softened the blow with a sympathetic explanation. The last thing she wanted was to face Cameron Ryder and pretend that she was unaware of his lies. She glanced at her watch.

She had exactly nine and a half hours to figure out a plan of action, exactly that long to decide whether she wanted to ignore his duplicity and continue seeing Cameron Ryder or put him out of her life forever. Neither alternative appealed in the least, but try as she might, she couldn't think of another.

"Out of one and a half million men, why did I have to spill coffee on *him*?" she muttered.

NINA LAY ON THE SOFA in her darkened apartment and stared at the clock on the VCR. She'd been counting down the minutes until Cameron Ryder's arrival, waiting for the buzz of her intercom. Though she expected the nerve-jangling sound, she still winced and covered her ears when it came.

She should have been looking forward to their date, anticipating another wonderful night with a man she found endlessly fascinating. Instead, she was dressed in her rattiest sweats, curled up on the sofa with a pint of Häagen-Dazs. Though the ice cream could never replace a date with a handsome man, right now she was willing to give the ice cream a fair shot. She'd already downed half the carton of Dulce de Leche and managed to work up a decent case of righteous indignation.

She should be more upset, even furious. The guy had used her! Though she'd tried to conjure a memory that fit that scenario, she couldn't. He'd casually asked her about her job, but hadn't pressed for more. If he really was interested in inside information, he wasn't much of spy. "Yeah," Nina muttered, shoving another spoonful of ice cream in her mouth. "You just blabbered everything. Loose lips sink ships."

The buzzer sounded again and Nina wondered how long it would take before Cameron Ryder realized she'd stood him up. Would she be worth just two rings? Or would she merit more? There must be some standardized gauge for these things, she mused. Now that would be a good idea for a story in *Attitudes.* If he got to four rings of her buzzer, that meant that he must really like her. Five rings would make him totally infatuated and well on the way to falling in love. She could do a survey.

She sat silently for a long moment, waiting for the third ring. When it didn't come, a wave of disappointment washed over her. So maybe she did like him a little more than he liked her. Nina flopped back on the sofa and gobbled another spoonful of the ice cream. He'd probably try calling or maybe even come back in an hour. But as far as Nina was concerned it was over. Mr. Right had become Mr. Wrong.

Nina took one last spoonful of ice cream, but the spoon stopped halfway to her mouth when a knock sounded at the door. Frantic, she jumped up from the sofa and hurried toward the door. But on the way, she stubbed her toe on the coffee table.

The pain was excruciating, so bad that Nina cried out. She slapped her hand over her mouth and rubbed her little toe with her other hand, hopping up and down on one foot. But the ice cream carton she'd dropped had created a slick spot on the hardwood floor and her one foot flew out from under her. She landed with a thud, a sound followed by a string of silent curses.

"Nina? Are you in there?" He knocked again. "Nina?"

Grimacing, she crawled over to the door and put her face down against floor. Drawing a shaky breath, she said the only thing left to say. *"Meow."* Though it didn't sound much like a cat, she hoped the door might muffle it into an acceptable likeness.

"Nina?"

"Meow," she replied. She breathed a sigh of relief when she heard his footsteps retreat down the hall. Nina leaned back against the door and rubbed her sore

backside. None of this would have been necessary had she come up with a decision regarding Cameron Ryder. Even though her heart told her to open the door and throw herself into his arms, her head told her that a job in editorial could be hers if she played her cards right.

She closed her eyes and tried to picture him—finely pressed trousers, a sweater that molded to his muscular torso, and that leather jacket he wore so well. She'd been too frightened to take a look through the peephole in the door, somehow certain he'd know she was on the other side, sure that one look at him would cause her resolve to crumble. The thought that she might never see him again brought a twinge of regret, but maybe she was better off this way.

Or maybe he'd buy the magazine and he'd be her new boss. Then she'd see him every day! With a soft groan, Nina struggled to her feet. She reached back and flipped on the lights but another knock on the door caused her to flip them back off. Pressing her palms on either side of the peephole, she squinted through it. Now two men stood outside her door—Cameron, dressed in a beautifully tailored suit, and Rocco Campinelli, wearing a pair of tattered overalls.

"Miss Forrester? Are you in there? Is everything all right?"

"Gee, he must really like me to bring the landlord up here," she murmured beneath her breath. Mr. Campinelli, a robust Italian and an incredible cook, lived in an apartment on the first floor. From there, he coordinated repairs, received packages, dispensed advice and made pasta that caused her mouth to water whenever she walked into the building.

"I heard a thud and then I heard her cat meowing," Cameron explained.

"She doesn't have a cat," the landlord answered. "No pets in my building. It's against the rules." A key jangled in the lock.

Nina slowly backed away from the door. They weren't going to come in, were they? The first lock clicked and she scurried over to the bedroom door. The second lock clicked and she dove for the floor. When she heard the door swing open, Nina scrambled beneath the bed and held her breath.

The lights in her apartment came on and she heard Cameron and Mr. Campinelli step inside. "It doesn't look like she's home."

"I heard something," Cameron insisted. "I just want to make sure everything is all right."

Nina peered out from beneath the dust ruffle. Cameron casually strolled through her living room, taking in the surroundings. No matter what he wore, he always looked good, so good she could barely take her eyes off him. His jacket accented his wide shoulders and the pants made his waist and hips look impossibly narrow. He stopped at the ice cream carton on the floor between the bedroom and the sofa, the ever-growing puddle of melted Häagen-Dazs a little hard to ignore.

"She has quite a decorating flair, doesn't she?" Mr. Campinelli commented. "All this fifties' stuff was considered junk just a few years back. Look at this table, formica with the little boomerangs. Me and the missus had a table just like this when we got married."

Nina had slaved over the decoration of her apartment, haunted second-hand shops and flea markets for the perfect accessories with just the right amount of kitsch appeal. The walls were painted in bright colors and nothing really matched but Nina liked it that way. Nina considered the rules of interior decoration the same as the rules of fashion—they were meant to be broken regularly. Besides, the fifties' and sixties' and seventies' stuff was always so cheap, how could she resist?

"It's very...original," Cameron said. "I've never seen anything quite like it."

"I'm not sure if Nina has it this way because she likes it or because she thinks it's funny. She's an odd one. Have you noticed the way she dresses?"

Cameron chuckled. "I kind of like the way she dresses."

"Well, it doesn't look like she's here."

"What about this ice cream?" Cameron said, squatting to pick up the carton. "It's still cold." He glanced around, looking right into the bedroom to where she was hidden. She closed her eyes, as if that would keep him from seeing her.

When she opened them again, she watched Cameron and Mr. Campinelli head toward the kitchen. She used the opportunity to find a better hiding place. Crawling on her stomach, she made her way to the bathroom, then scrambled to her feet and hid inside the narrow linen closet. She could just see the bed from the crack between the door and the jamb and Nina waited, praying that he'd finally leave.

But he didn't and when light flooded the bathroom,

she held her breath, knowing full well she was about to be discovered. The closet door pulled open in front of her and Nina pasted a smile on her face as she looked up into Cameron Ryder's green eyes.

"IF I WERE THE suspicious type, I'd think you were avoiding me," Cameron said. He grinned and crooked his finger. "Come on out."

"What are you doing here?" she murmured.

"What are you doing in there?" he asked.

"In here? Oh, I was just...folding some towels."

Cameron watched as she patted a stack of colorful wash cloths. She was dressed in faded sweats and her hair was tumbled around her face. Though some might have called it messy, he thought it looked incredibly sexy. When she rearranged the last of the towels, she reluctantly stepped out of the tiny closet.

"We had a date," he said. Cam looked into her face and a warm flood of affection washed over him. He'd only been away from her for a day, yet he'd missed her. Thinking about her never really lived up to being with her—being close enough to touch her, to stare into her pretty blue eyes, to listen to her musical laugh.

He bent closer to brush a kiss across her lips, but she turned away. "Was that tonight?" she asked with mock innocence. She strolled out of the bathroom into the bedroom.

Cameron frowned, startled by her cool rebuff. She looked tired and a little on edge. "You know it was," he said, following after her. "What's this all about? Why aren't you ready?"

What kind of game was she playing? Last night

they'd agreed to dinner, right before he'd dropped her off. He'd made a reservation at Le Cirque, the best table in the restaurant. He'd even ordered a chocolate soufflé for dessert. And after that he'd planned a ride through Central Park in a carriage. And after that he'd planned to tell her the truth. Right after he told her she was the most incredible woman he'd ever met.

Mr. Campinelli poked his head in the bedroom. "You all right, Nina? You know this guy?"

Nina forced a smile, then nodded. "I'm fine, Mr. Campinelli. Just fine. You can go now."

The landlord looked at them both, then nodded and quietly let himself out. Nina raked her hand through her rumpled hair. "There's a good question," she muttered under her breath. "Do I know this guy? How would I answer that?" She turned away, then busied herself making the bed, straightening the covers and fluffing the pillows.

"Are you sick?" Cameron asked, concern lacing his tone.

"No."

"Working?" he asked.

She sent him a suspicious glance. "Why would you want to know about my work?" she demanded.

Cameron frowned. This was not a mood he'd ever seen Nina in. She was normally so cheerful. Maybe she *was* sick. Her face seemed a bit flushed and the dark circles under her eyes didn't look good. "I just thought you might be avoiding me," he said.

She answered with a shake of her head and continued to meticulously smooth the bedspread. Impatient, he took her hand and pulled her from the bedroom to the living room sofa. Better to get them as far away from the bed as possible since he'd need all his wits about him to figure out why she was acting this way. "Sit down."

Nina did as she was told, now smoothing her hands over the stained front of her sweatshirt before plucking fuzz from her sweatpants. "I really don't have time for—"

"If you didn't want to go out tonight, you should have just told me," Cameron said. An image of high school flashed in his mind, the cheerleader he'd called for a date. She'd never returned his call. It had taken him a long time to realize that she wasn't going to call back. Then he'd been stupid enough to ask her for a date in the hallway between classes. Was Nina trying to give him the brush-off as well?

His thoughts jumped to the weekend, to the moments they'd spent together in her bed. He couldn't have misread the desire he saw in her eyes. It had been there, so clear and urgent. "We can be honest with each other."

"Of course we can," Nina said brightly. "I just have other things on my mind. You know, the Cameron Ryder thing." She stared at him for a long moment, her gaze shrewd, probing. "That ruthless bastard who wants to ruin my life and my career? Remember him?"

His breath caught in his chest. *She knows*, Cameron thought. Somewhere, in her research, she'd come across something that made the connection clear. "Maybe I can help," he murmured, hoping that she'd take the opening. A long silence grew between them and he waited, wanting her to confront him, hoping that the deception would finally be over. "Go ahead," he said. "Ask me anything."

Nina sighed restlessly, then quickly stood. "I really do have to get back to work. We'll have to have dinner another night."

He grabbed her hand and idly began to play with her fingers. "You can't work all day and all night. You need to take a break. Come on," he said, pulling her along to the bedroom, "we'll take a walk and then stop for some dinner. Nothing fancy."

Nina shook her head, then glanced down at what she was wearing. "I'm really not dressed for—"

"I'll wait," Cameron said. He stepped back from her, every shred of common sense telling him he should keep walking, out of her apartment, out of her building and into the street. He felt as if he were sitting in a pool of gasoline and Nina was flicking matches in his direction. But something told him that it would be the worst mistake of his life to let her go without a fight. She was the best thing that had happened to him in a very long time, maybe ever. "I'll wait," he repeated, this time more softly.

He closed the bedroom door behind him, then slowly wandered her apartment. Like the clothes she wore, the apartment suited her. The furniture was so absurd it was almost art, the colors bright and the forms just unusual enough to make them interesting. And beneath it all was a casual disregard for the strictures of trends and fashions. Had he looked at a thousand different apartments in Manhattan, he would have known this was Nina's.

He stared at his reflection in a mirror and straightened his tie, then strolled over to a bookshelf near the kitchen. The shelves were filled with hundreds of troll dolls, each one more bizarre than the next. He picked up a naked troll with electric blue hair.

"They're strange, aren't they?"

He turned to find her standing behind him. She'd changed into a simple sweater and a pair of jeans. Her hair was tied loosely back in a scarf. It always amazed him that every time he looked at her, she became more and more beautiful. "They are," he agreed. "Cute and a little frightening at the same time."

"Actually, they're an acquired taste. I find them in the strangest places but every time I see one, I have to buy it. For luck." Picking one up, she shrugged indifferently. "I guess they don't always work." She tossed the troll back onto the shelf and walked away.

Cameron carefully put the doll back in its place, then turned to her. She was not going to make this easy. She had every intention of making him pay and pay dearly. He just wished she'd get on with it. "Are you ready to go?"

Nina grabbed a jacket from the closet and started toward the door. "Let's go."

Cam caught up to her and grabbed her hand, lacing his fingers through hers. If he only knew what she was thinking. He cursed silently. Why had he even lied to her in the first place? He should have just told her that the man she'd been assigned to investigate was the man she'd dumped coffee on.

Then again, maybe he was reading her all wrong. Maybe telling her he was Cameron Ryder wasn't the most sensible thing to do. Hell, he really didn't know what she was angry about. To him, women were a mystery. She could be mad because he hadn't called her today, or because he'd been a few minutes late. Or maybe she was angry because he hadn't accepted her offer and made love to her.

And if she did suspect the truth, it left her with no option but to refuse to see him. Maybe he should just give her time to work this all out in her head. "So, how is your project going at work?" he said in a feeble attempt at small talk.

"We always talk about me," she said coolly as she descended the stairs to the ground floor. "Why don't you tell me about *your* work?"

"I'm sure you wouldn't be interested," he countered. "I'd rather talk about you. How's your project going?"

With a soft curse, she yanked open the front door and stepped outside. The door nearly struck him in the face and he was forced to drop her hand to protect himself. He caught up with her at the bottom of the steps and grabbed her hand. "All right. Let's just get it all out, right here, right now," he said.

"What's that?" she asked, a defiant look in her eyes.

"Do you want to say it or should I?"

"I don't have any idea what you're talking about," Nina replied, her expression showing veiled hostility.

"You were right that night in the coffee shop. Cameron Ryder is a bastard."

She clenched her fists and stared up into his face. "And how could you possibly know that?" she asked, her eyes narrow and bright with anger.

"Because he lied to you. He was afraid if you knew

who he really was then you wouldn't have anything to do with him. And from the first time he saw you, he wanted to be with you. So he did something really stupid and he deceived you. And since that moment he's wanted to tell you, but he's been afraid he'd lose you. And he's very, very, *very* sorry."

"And how do you know all this?" She tipped up her chin defiantly, the color high in her cheeks. "Are you two friends? Business associates?"

"You know how I know it," Cam said. "I'm not sure how *you* know, but you know."

"Say it," Nina said. "I want to hear you say it."

"I'm Cameron Ryder," he said.

He didn't see it coming, had no time to prepare. When her fist hit his stomach, all the air rushed from his lungs. She'd hit him, not very hard but in exactly the right spot in his solar plexus, and for a moment he couldn't catch his breath. He tried to speak, but nothing came out except a slow groan. Bent over in pain, he waited for his breathing to start again.

Her punch startled her as much as it had him. "Oh—oh, I'm sorry," she cried. Cameron felt her hand patting his back. "I didn't mean to hit you so—are you all right? I'm sorry. I thought you'd—"

He held out his hand. "I'm fine," he wheezed.

She grabbed him by the lapels of his jacket and yanked him up to face her. "Good," she snapped. "Because if I never see you again, it won't be too—" She paused, frowning. "If I ever see you again, it will be too—" Nina cursed softly. "You know what I mean!" She turned on her heel and started off in the opposite direction down the sidewalk.

Cam hurried after her, rubbing his stomach and trying to grab a little oxygen. "Nina, I'm sorry. I deserved that and if it makes you feel better, then you can punch me again."

She turned around and came after him, but Cam backed away. "I should!" she cried. "How could you do that to me?"

"I told you, I—"

"Not that," Nina cried. "I know why you lied. How could you—we nearly—we almost—in my bed at the inn. Or have you forgotten?"

"Damn it, Nina, how could I ever forget? I haven't been able to stop thinking about you since that moment. I can still smell your hair and feel your skin. The taste of your mouth is still on mine. I stopped because I didn't want you to regret it later, once you found out who I really was. I didn't want you to hate me."

"Well, you were wrong. I do hate you."

"No, you don't," Cam said.

"Yes, I do."

He took a few steps toward her, closing the distance between them. "No, you don't. And I can prove it." He took her face between his hands and tipped it up. And then he kissed her, long and deep, moving over her mouth until he felt every last bit of her resistance melt. She couldn't deny him this, the desire they shared, no matter how angry she was. When he drew away, he looked down into her eyes, satisfied that the kiss had affected her as much as it had him.

"I should punch you again," she murmured.

He held out his hands in surrender. "Feel free. As long as I can kiss you again."

"So what does that prove?" Nina asked. "You're a proficient kisser. Maybe so good you could make a marble statue go weak at the knees. But that doesn't mean I forgive you. You tricked me."

"Nina, that was me in your bed. Maybe you didn't know my real name, but that was still me."

She shook her head. "Do you think everything can be the same now that I know you're Cameron Ryder? You're trying to take over *Attitudes*."

"That has nothing to do with us."

"You're right," Nina replied. "Because there is no us." With that, she spun on her heel and headed back toward her building. Cameron had no choice but to follow, but when he caught up to her and tried to grab her arm, she evaded his grasp.

"If you want me to knock you over, just try that again," she warned.

"Fine. But I'm not going to give up," he said. "And I'll take a rain check on dinner."

This time he was the one who turned and walked away, leaving her standing on the sidewalk. He didn't bother to glance back, though he was sorely tempted to take just one look. Hell, he wanted to rush right back to her and yank her into his arms and kiss her until she surrendered. But Nina was spoiling for a fight and he wasn't going to give it to her. Instead, he'd give her time to cool off and then he'd try again.

Cameron sucked in a deep breath of the crisp evening air. God, she'd tasted good. In such a short time, he'd grown to love the way she felt in his arms, the sweet sensation of her mouth beneath his. He wanted Nina Forrester and he was going to do whatever it took to convince her that she wanted him. He just hoped it wouldn't take long.

Because there was only one way to describe what Nina did to him: she took his breath away. And she didn't even need to punch him in the gut to do it.

5

Nɪɴᴀ ʜᴀᴅ ᴛʜᴏᴜɢʜᴛ very seriously about calling in sick to work. After the events of last night, she wasn't sure she could even pull herself out of bed, much less drag herself to the office. And she hadn't even overdosed on chocolate! But she had work waiting for her—a fact check on an article about calorie-burning sex and a meeting with the magazine's lawyers regarding liability on an article called "Mosh Pit Survival Techniques." And then there was always her research on Cameron Ryder.

Doubts about her decision to walk away from Cameron had kept her up all night long. Though, technically, he'd walked away from her, she'd done her best to make that happen. So she'd spent the wee hours of the morning rearranging and cataloguing her troll doll collection, cleaning her refrigerator, and sweeping up the flock of dust bunnies she'd noticed under her bed when she'd been hiding there. But nothing she'd tried to occupy herself with could stop her thoughts from going right back to Cameron.

Though he'd left her standing on the sidewalk, when she got back upstairs to her apartment, she'd risked a peek through the blinds, hoping that he'd reconsidered and come back. But the street was empty. Earlier in the evening, she'd been worth two rings of the bell, a couple of knocks at the door, and a call to the landlord. Now, she was barely worth a few moments on an empty street.

Why had she let herself believe he was Mr. Right? Experience should have told her that falling in love with a man after just a few days was a recipe for disaster. But he'd been so sweet...and so incredibly sexy. Nina moaned softly. She'd let her hormones overwhelm her common sense, a condition that seemed chronic in his presence. Even in the midst of their argument, she'd been tempted to throw herself into his arms and kiss the anger away.

But now she'd have to convince herself that she'd been wrong about him, that Cameron Ryder had turned from Mr. Right to Mr. Wrong as quickly as lettuce turned to green slime in her refrigerator.

Her words came back to her in remarkable clarity: *If I never see you again it will be too soon!* Or something to that effect. Those double negatives always gave her fits. Even so, maybe she shouldn't have been so determined to toss him out of her life. He considered their circumstances merely coincidental and not so important that they'd ruin their relationship.

Whether he was Jack or Cameron, his feelings hadn't changed. And deep inside her heart, Nina's really hadn't either. Drawing a deep breath, she tugged her jacket more tightly around her and hurried toward the office. Where were her loyalties supposed to lie? If Cameron took over the magazine, Nina was sure it would be run better than it ever had been before. But Charlotte had given Nina her first real job, providing an escape from an awful string of odd jobs that added nothing to her résumé. And even though her boss could barely remember Nina's name, she still owed Charlotte and her co-workers a tiny bit of loyalty, didn't she?

If only she could just step back and let the battle for *Attitudes* rage on. Then after it was over, she could declare her allegiance to whomever was left standing. Nina pushed through the glass door and stepped into the lobby.

"Morning, Nina," Kathy called. "Hey, great work on that Ryder deal. Everyone is so excited."

Nina frowned then nodded. Since when did Kathy concern herself with Nina's research work? Obviously Charlotte had been spreading positive propaganda using Nina's sketchy memo on Cameron Ryder. She punched the button for the elevator and when the doors opened, Doug and Greg, music critics for the magazine, stepped out.

"Hey, Nina!" Greg cried. "Way to go with Ryder."

"Charlotte says with your help we should be in the clear," Doug added. "It's the first time I've seen her smile since this whole thing started."

Nina gave them a little wave as she stepped on the elevator. By the time she reached the third floor, she was thoroughly confused. And that confusion only grew as she made her way to her office, past co-workers who all sent their congratulations and good wishes her way. She quickly slipped inside her office and closed the door behind her, feeling as if she'd been caught in one of those episodes of *The Twilight Zone*, as if something in the world had changed while she slept and no one had bothered to tell her. Nina sighed. Only she hadn't slept last night.

"It's about time!"

Nina jumped, pressing her hand to her heart. Lizbeth sat in Nina's chair, her designer pumps propped up on the edge of Nina's desk.

"What are you doing in here?"

"I'm waiting for you," Lizbeth said. "What have you done with your hair? It looks like that ball of fuzz I pull out of my vacuum cleaner every year or so."

Nina ignored the gibe. "Is it a strange morning or what? Everyone is acting so weird."

Lizbeth sent her a weak smile. "Hmm. You noticed that?"

Nodding, she hung her coat up on the hook on the back of the door. Then she turned back to her friend and noticed the guilty look on her face. "What's wrong? Charlotte didn't decide to sell, did she?"

"No," Lizbeth replied, slowly shaking her head. "Honey, after what I told her, I don't think she'll be selling anytime soon."

"You talked with Charlotte?"

With her gaze firmly fixed on her manicure, Lizbeth hesitantly explained. "I just want you to understand. Charlotte was so despondent and needy and she trapped me in the ladies' room and started weeping. And I know how much you want that job in editorial so I..."

"What? What did you do?" Nina demanded.

"I told her about Jack—I mean, Cameron Ryder. I just let it slip in conversation and she grabbed onto it like a terrier with a T-bone steak."

A tightly held breath slipped from Nina's lips and she slowly lowered herself into a guest chair. "Lizbeth, that's my private business! What did you say to her? Did you tell her about our weekend together? That we nearly...you know..."

"Did the big nasty?" Lizbeth asked. "No. But I might have mentioned that you and Cameron Ryder had met. That you became intimate friends with him in order to enhance your research for the magazine. And that you might be able to use your influence with him to stop his takeover of the magazine. Or at least slow it down until Charlotte can convince her father to give her more money."

Nina stared at her, wide-eyed and incredulous. "I can't believe this."

"I also mentioned your interest in that position in editorial." She swung her feet to the floor. "Honey, you have a chance here to make your dreams come true."

"Lizbeth, what have you done? That's only if Charlotte manages to keep this magazine afloat. You don't know Cameron Ryder. The man is ruthless."

Lizbeth smiled slyly. "But you do know him, honey. And he's your ticket to editorial."

"He might have been, except I sent him packing last night. And after what I said to him, he won't be back. In truth, I was so adamant, he might just have to relocate to the suburbs to avoid seeing me again."

"Well, you better get him back," Lizbeth warned. "Apologize, grovel, bat your baby blues. Whatever you do, you need Cameron Ryder back in your life."

"You want me to go back to—"

Her words were interrupted when the door to

Nina's office swung open and Charlotte Danforth swooped inside. "Nina, darling," she gushed. She hurried to Nina's side and gave her a little air kiss on each cheek. "Lizbeth told me the marvelous news. When I asked you to learn everything you could about Cameron Ryder, I never expected you'd go so far. You're a real team player, Nina."

Nina held out her hand to stem the flow of compliments. "Charlotte, I think I should tell you—"

"Oh, now, don't be humble. All of us at *Attitudes* owe you a great measure of thanks." Her expression turned hard. "With your help, we'll squash that Cameron Ryder like the cockroach he is."

Nina sent Lizbeth an aggravated look, but her friend had pasted on her very best smile for Charlotte's benefit. "Just like a bug," Lizbeth drawled.

Charlotte grabbed Nina's hand and pulled her from her chair. "Come along, Nina. You and I are going to lunch. We'll discuss strategy over lobster salads and martinis. And Lizbeth tells me you have some ideas for editorial. I'd love to hear those as well. I just haven't been able to find someone for that assistant's position. Maybe you're my girl?"

"Lunch?" Nina glanced around her office. "But it's only nine o'clock."

"Then we'll go shopping!" Charlotte cried. "You do like to shop, don't you?"

Nina nodded. Though the thought of shopping with Charlotte was daunting at best, at least the woman was calling her by the correct name. She ought to consider herself lucky. This was a very big step.

"What do you think? First we'll get coffee. I know

this wonderful shop on Lex that has a to-die-for Italian roast. And then we'll hit Bloomies and Saks and Lord and Taylor. And while we shop, we'll really get to know each other. Won't that be nice, Nina? And I have a standing lunch reservation at L'Auberge. You do like French bistro food, don't you?" She smiled. "Of course you do. Who wouldn't?"

With that, Charlotte turned and swept out of the office. She didn't realize that Nina hadn't followed until she was halfway down the hall. "Come along, Nina!" she called.

Nina shook her finger at Lizbeth. "You will pay for this," she warned before she ran after her boss. She caught up with her in Charlotte's office. Charlotte pointed to a chair and Nina dutifully sat down.

"Now, we have to develop a strategy," Charlotte said, pacing back and forth behind her desk as she puffed on one of her French cigarettes. "I need to know exactly how much he plans to offer. I'm lining up some interim financing to cover our debts and I have to be sure my deal is better than his deal. Otherwise Daddy will..." She laughed lightly. "Well, that's not your concern."

Charlotte grabbed a plastic Blockbuster bag from her credenza and handed it to Nina. "You can start with these," she suggested.

Nina dumped the bag on Charlotte's desk and five videos tumbled out. "What are these?"

"Old James Bond movies. I want you to study these. If you're going to spy for me, you need to know what you're doing. Pussy Galore and Plenty O'Toole are experts in the field of feminine espionage."

"I—I'm supposed to learn from a woman named Pussy Galore?" Nina asked.

"Just her name alone made men fall at her feet," Charlotte said with a sigh. "Use your charms, your feminine wiles. He's obviously interested, Nina. Turn up the heat and see what jumps out of the pan."

Charlotte grabbed her coat and her purse, then headed to the door. "Come along now. We have shopping to do. We have to buy you a whole new wardrobe. You'll never be able to seduce a man in that outfit."

Nina jumped up and hurried after Charlotte. But her thoughts weren't on shopping or lobster salad or even Pussy Galore. Instead, Nina was thinking about the next time she'd see Cameron Ryder. Even though she'd vowed never to see him again, circumstances had changed. By letting her go so easily last night on the sidewalk, Cameron had dealt a major blow to her ego. Now she had a chance to regain some of her lost pride—and secure the job she'd been coveting.

And maybe, along the way, she might have a chance to kiss him just one more time.

RUSH HOUR TRAFFIC was gridlocked uptown and it took the cab nearly an hour to go from Lord and Taylors to Nina's apartment in the East Village. Charlotte had paid for the ride and when the cab finally pulled up in front of the building, Nina tumbled out of the back seat with her boxes and bags.

As she'd expected, the day had been exhausting, both physically and mentally. Charlotte had insisted on buying her a new wardrobe, one that was meant en-

tirely for seduction. She'd also insisted that Nina wear
a sexy little black dress out of the store, a body-
skimming number with a low neckline and a high
hemline. She'd also tucked an address into Nina's
pocket for one of Charlotte's society parties, ordering
Nina to meet her there later that evening for another
strategy session.

Hefting the bags and boxes up under her arms, she
wearily climbed the front steps to her building. It was
nearly eight. All she wanted right now was a hot bath
and a warm bed.

"Miss Forrester?"

The voice came out of nowhere and Nina jumped.
When she turned around she noticed, for the first time,
the limo parked across the street. A uniformed driver
stood at the curb beneath a street lamp. She brushed
the hair out of her eyes and tried to still her hammering
heart. "Yes. I'm Nina Forrester."

He hurried up and took the bags from her hands.
"I've been asked to pick you up."

Nina shook her head. "No," she moaned. "Can't you
just tell Charlotte that you didn't see me, that I didn't
answer my door?"

"I was told not to leave until I'd convinced you to
come."

Nina sighed and shook her head. Her sudden friend-
ship with Charlotte Danforth was beginning to wear
thin already! They'd spent the entire day together,
shopping and chatting, as if Nina had suddenly become an important part of Charlotte's social circle. Her
boss had even discussed editorial ideas over happy
hour cocktails at one of those trendy bars that the city's

social elite frequented. And if that wasn't enough, now she'd have to make small talk at some silly party.

"All right," she said. "But you have to promise that you'll wait for me. I'm only going to stay for an hour."

The driver nodded, then took the rest of her packages and headed toward the car. When she'd settled herself in the back seat, the driver circled the block and started uptown through evening traffic. Nina reached down and slipped off her shoes, then rubbed her aching feet. She'd been so busy all day long that she'd barely had time to think about Cameron Ryder. Tucking her toes beneath her, she glanced around the car. "Another ride in a limo," she said with a tired smile. "This is getting to be a habit."

Though she'd agreed in principle to go along with Charlotte's plan, putting the plan into action was another matter entirely. Sure, it might be a simple task to seduce a man and get him to spill all his secrets, but Cameron wasn't just any man. He had the unique ability to turn seduction right back on her, to touch her until she shivered and to whisper provocative words in her ear that made her lose all her common sense.

Nina closed her eyes and tipped her head back, trying to push all thought of Cameron from her mind. But unbidden images invaded her brain. With a soft curse, she opened her eyes and leaned forward to rummage through the limo's refrigerator. It had been stocked with soda and snacks, exactly what she needed to soothe her nerves. Nina grabbed a package of potato chips and stretched out on the seat, munching as the traffic moved around them.

When the limo finally stopped, she glanced outside

to find them parked on Riverside Drive. She scrambled to put on her shoes and tug on the ever-rising hemline of her new dress. Raking her fingers through her hair, she tried to work up the energy needed to keep up with her boss's hard partying image, but a Coke and potato chips provided precious little energy. She managed a bright smile for the driver as he escorted her up to the front door. The doorman let her inside and directed her to the elevator and Apartment 703.

But when she got to the door, the hallway and the apartment were silent. No music, no sound of chattering voices. The door of 703 was slightly ajar. She knocked and it swung open in front of her. Inside, the apartment was dimly lit, candles casting soft illumination against the walls. "Hello? Charlotte?"

A figure stepped out of the darkness beyond the windows. Nina's heart skipped a beat and a tiny gasp slipped from her lips. "Jack!"

"Cameron," he reminded her, his lips quirking into an apologetic smile. He slowly walked towards her, his hands shoved in his pockets. He wore faded jeans and a body-hugging sweater that clung to his muscular torso. "I was hoping you'd come."

"This is *your* apartment?"

He nodded.

Nina glanced around. In comparison, her place looked like a well-decorated walk-in closet. His living room was the size of her entire apartment. High ceilings and rich woodwork added to an elegant decor. Windows overlooked the Hudson, boasting a view of stunning sunsets. No traffic sounds drifted up from the street and all Nina could hear was the soft sound of music drifting from the stereo.

Her first impulse was to turn and run, to hop right back inside the limo and head back downtown. But as she met his gaze, a tiny shiver skittered up her spine. Wasn't this what she was waiting for? An opportunity to put her spying plan to work? Drawing a ragged breath, she casually slipped out of her coat and dropped it on a nearby chair. The dress got the expected reaction and his gaze slowly raked her body. "Why did you bring me here?" she asked.

Cameron crossed the room, his movements lithe, almost predatory. Once again, Nina's instincts told her to run. She already knew her resolve could disappear with just one touch of his hand. But as long as she kept focussed, he couldn't intimidate her or frighten her. She just had to remember why she was here.

"I figured you wouldn't take my calls and you wouldn't see me at your apartment. And I wanted to talk to you without any interruptions."

"You lied to me," Nina said, defiantly staring into his dark eyes. "I don't need to listen to you."

His gaze was unwavering and so intense she knew he could see into her soul. Could he tell she still wanted him? He took her hand in his and a tremor raced through her body. "If I'd told you who I was that night at the coffee shop, would you have agreed to see me again?"

"I guess we'll never know," Nina said.

Considering her new role as Mata Hari, she couldn't very well yank her hand from his. So where was she supposed to go from here? She hadn't had a chance to

watch the James Bond movies so she had no idea what
Pussy Galore would do in a situation like this, though
she could guess. She'd probably throw out her chest,
sashay up to the guy and wrap her well-toned limbs
around his body until he begged for mercy.

But Nina wasn't a Bond girl. She'd never intention-
ally seduced a man in her life and she was pretty sure
she didn't want to. Just an attempt might bring on a
bout of hyperventilation that would ruin the effect.
"I—I'll have some of that wine," she said, pointing to
the bottle on the dining room table.

Without taking his eyes off her, Cameron moved
back to the table. He deftly removed the cork, then
poured a goblet full for Nina. He splashed a bit in his
glass, then returned to her side.

Drawing a deep breath, Nina took a huge gulp of the
wine, hoping it would soothe her nerves. But when
there was no immediate effect, she drank the rest of the
glass in short order.

"More?" he asked as he took the empty glass from
her hand.

She nodded, smoothing her palms over her dress. "I
have a question," she said.

"And I have all sorts of answers," he replied.

"Why *Attitudes*? Why not buy another magazine?"

He shrugged. "Because I want it," Cameron said.
"And usually when I want something, I do everything
in my power to get it."

He was talking about more than just business acquisitions, Nina suspected. "Do you want the magazine
more than you want me?" she asked, an indignant
edge in her voice.

"That's business. You're...pleasure."

Nina swallowed hard. "And—and you can separate the two?"

"I have to, Nina. And so do you." He slowly handed her the wineglass, his fingers brushing hers. The contact was brief, but electric, sending desire pulsing through her body. The need to touch him was acute, but she ignored it, choosing to wander around his apartment, picking up knickknacks and examining them for some clue to his character.

But there were very few personal items lying about. Everything was decorator perfect, as if he hadn't taken the time to personally select the elements that surrounded him. The only spot that seemed his own was a small corner desk that held a computer and was surrounded by papers and books. Nina sipped at her wine, noting that she ought to go through the papers at the first available opportunity. She smiled to herself. This spy turn wasn't so hard after all.

"So, what do you suggest?" she asked.

"I suggest we forget about work and concentrate on us," he replied.

She turned back to him, then perched herself on the edge of his desk. Her skirt had ridden up on her thighs, offering a tantalizing view and she slowly crossed her legs. He stared for a long moment and when he looked up, Nina smiled in satisfaction.

"Dinner," he murmured. "Have you had dinner?"

Nina pushed away from the desk and moved on to the bookshelves, lazily running her fingers along the spines of the texts. "I am a little hungry." His gaze followed her. She felt it, surprised that she could wield such power over him. For once, she felt the balance shift and she was the one in control.

"We could go out," he suggested.

"No," Nina said with a shrug. "I'd rather stay in. Why don't you cook me something?"

"I'm not much of a cook," he said. "But I guess I could try." He glanced around the room. "Why don't you relax and I'll go scare something up."

Nina watched as he walked out of the room to the kitchen. The moment he was out of sight, she set down her wineglass and hurried to the desk. Her heart slammed in her chest as she rifled through the papers. "What am I looking for?" she murmured. "I don't even know what I'm looking for. I should have brought one of those tiny little cameras they always have in the movies."

But after five minutes of searching, she gave up. There was nothing on his desk that made any sense to her at all. Every paper was filled with computer gobbledygook. Defeated in her first assignment as a spy, Nina grabbed her wine and walked over to the sofa to sit down.

Cameron had left the bottle on the coffee table and she filled her glass once more and took a healthy sip. Kicking her legs up on the sofa, she leaned back into the pillows. Exhaustion overwhelmed her and she closed her eyes as the sound of clanging pots drifted out of the kitchen. Odd, how the sound of Cameron moving about the apartment was soothing. Maybe it was the wine. Or maybe it was the knowledge that she could be around him without losing control. Or perhaps it was the simple fact that they were together again and he still cared. Nina sighed, allowing her thoughts to drift.

Yep, this spy business wasn't difficult at all.

CAMERON CAREFULLY arranged the fried chicken and Tater Tots on a plate. If only he had a few sprigs of parsley. That always made things look better. He shifted the Tater Tots to one side and rearranged the chicken. He should have sent out for Chinese or pizza. Two frozen TV dinners on fancy china weren't exactly gourmet fare.

But then, the meal didn't matter. Nina was here, with him, and she hadn't tried once to punch him. That was a positive step, he mused. He glanced down at the fried chicken. Although, she might feel differently once he put dinner in front of her.

"Dinner is served," Cam called as he walked out to the living room. But the room was silent. He glanced around and didn't see Nina anywhere. A soft curse slipped from his lips. Sometime during the twenty minutes he'd spent cooking up a storm, she'd snuck out of the apartment!

He should have been more aware of her state of mind. Yesterday, she wanted nothing to do with him. Feelings like that didn't change overnight. Alone and waiting for him to appear with dinner gave her the perfect opportunity to reflect on his actions. She was gone, and he might never get her back again.

An emptiness settled into his heart at the thought of never seeing her again. In such a short time, she'd become a part of his life, a reason to breathe, to get up in the morning. His life was no longer about work—it was about living, enjoying every minute of every day, anticipating the next time he'd look into her eyes.

He slowly circled the sofa, cursing his stupidity, only to find Nina curled up there, her hands tucked under her cheek and her body hugging a throw pillow. Quietly, Cam set the food down on the coffee table, then squatted down beside her, relief washing over him. For a long while, he watched her breathe, his gaze taking in the perfect features of her face.

He wasn't sure what to do. Given the choice, he could sit here all night watching her, listening to the tiny sounds she made as she slept. He reached out and brushed a silken tendril of hair from her face. Or he could scoop her up into his arms, carry her to his bed, and let nature take its course.

Nothing could cool his attraction for her—not her indifference, not his fear of losing her. The moment she'd walked in the door, a current raced between them, electric, magnetic, sparked by every look and every word, and fueled by the sexy dress she wore.

She couldn't stay angry forever. And he was willing to give her whatever time she needed. Besides, he really couldn't understand her concerns about the magazine. Once he'd purchased *Attitudes,* she could have any job on the staff she wanted. Hell, he'd make her editor-in-chief if that's what she wanted.

He'd give her anything to assure himself of a future with her. He chuckled softly. If someone had told him he'd be feeling this way about a woman after less than a week, he would have laughed in their face. But then, he'd never anticipated meeting a woman like Nina. If there was one woman for every man, then he had to believe Nina Forrester was meant for him.

Suddenly, he needed to hear her voice, to hear her say that she felt the same—that once she got past her anger, they still had a future together. Cam ran a finger along her cheek. "Nina? Sweetheart, wake up."

Her eyes fluttered, then opened. At first she looked confused, as if she wasn't sure where she was. Then she gave him a sleepy smile. "What are you doing here?" she said.

"You're in my apartment," he said, still stroking her face. "Do you want to stay? Or should I take you home?"

"Umm," she said. "I'm just a little tired. I had a very busy day. Just a few minutes and I'll...rest my eyes...sleep...just a few minutes."

He sat back on his heels and then noticed the nearly empty bottle of wine on the coffee table. "Just a little too much Merlot," he said with a soft chuckle.

She looked so sweet and vulnerable, curled up on his sofa in her oh-so sexy dress. When she'd tossed aside her coat earlier, he'd nearly moaned out loud at the sight of her, soft fabric clinging to every curve of her body, the neckline of her dress dipping precariously low. He'd immediately thought of that night at the inn, when she'd brushed aside her robe and asked him to make love to her.

As he had that night, he wanted to lose himself exploring that smooth expanse of skin, the gentle swell of her flesh and the cleft between her breasts. His fingers clenched and Cam drew a ragged breath. Now was not the time to be considering seduction.

Still, there was no denying his feelings for her. When he thought about his future, he thought about Nina. No other woman had captivated him the way she had, twisting him around her little finger. He'd never been in love before, never truly fallen hard for a woman. But he knew this was what it was like, this constant and unchanging need to be near her.

He reached out and captured a strand of her hair between his fingers. Leaving her here on his sofa to sleep was a temptation he'd have a hard time resisting. He should wake her and send her home. But Cam wanted her close by. They'd fashioned a truce of sorts and having her near made him more hopeful that the truce might turn into a surrender of sorts.

"What am I going to do with you?" he murmured. He reached over to the arm of the sofa and grabbed a soft cashmere throw, something his interior designer insisted on yet he'd never used. He was grateful for it now. Carefully, he drew the throw over her long legs, the sweet curve of her hip and her bare arms.

When his gaze drifted back to her face, she was staring at him through sleepy eyes. She smiled winsomely. "You're a handsome guy," she said, as if she'd just realized it. He wasn't sure whether she was awake or talking in her sleep.

His eyes fixed on her mouth and he fought the urge to kiss her. "And you're the most beautiful woman I've ever seen."

"Am I as beautiful as Pussy Galore?" she asked, her voice still slightly giddy from the wine.

Cam gasped. "Who?"

"Umm, she's a spy. I'm a spy. Charlotte told me I have to be a spy to save the magazine."

"And who are you spying on?" Cam asked, leaning closer.

Nina giggled softly. "Why you, of course. I'm going to stop you from buying the magazine," she sighed, "and ruining my life."

"I'd never do that," Cam murmured as he pulled the throw around her shoulders.

"She bought me all sorts of clothes. Do you like my dress? Charlotte calls it a 'seduce me' dress. Those aren't her exact words, but you get the picture, don't you? Would you like to seduce me?"

Now Cam was certain she didn't know what she was saying. The wine and exhaustion had taken a toll on her inhibitions. And though the offer was tempting, he knew better than to believe she really meant what she'd said. Just last night, she'd told him to take a hike. Now she claimed she wanted him to take her to bed.

"I think we'll leave that until later," Cam said.

"Okay," Nina agreed. "And I think I'll go back to sleep now." She closed her eyes and a few minutes later, her breathing grew deep and even.

Cam bent forward and pressed a gentle kiss on her forehead. Then he stood and walked over to his desk. A soft oath slipped from his lips and he raked his hand through his hair, unable to believe what he'd just heard.

Charlotte Danforth hadn't been his favorite person in the world, but now he really couldn't stand her. How dare she put Nina in such a position? How dare she take advantage of Nina's sweet nature? Hell, the woman could barely remember Nina's name and she had the audacity to use her in such a manner.

Over the past few days, Cam had seriously considered withdrawing his offer to buy the magazine. But now he was even more determined to take it over and to bounce Charlotte Danforth out on her sorry little butt. He snatched up the phone, then punched in a number, not bothering to consider the time.

When Jeff Myers answered, Cam got right to business. "I want you to make another offer to Charlotte Danforth. This time up the ante. I don't want to waste any more time. I want that magazine." With that, he hung up, certain that his orders would be followed.

He and Nina were never going to move on to their future until this whole magazine deal was signed and sealed. Cam wandered back to the sofa. He should go to bed; he had an early day tomorrow. But he was loath to leave Nina. So instead, Cam pulled an overstuffed leather chair closer to the sofa and sat down.

He'd just watch her for a little while. And if she woke up and wanted to go home, he'd take her. If she wanted something to eat, he'd feed her. And if she wanted something else...well, he'd cross that bridge when he came to it.

6

THE THROBBING IN HER HEAD was part of a dream. Someone was playing the "1812 Overture" in her bedroom closet and every time the cymbals crashed her head felt as if it was going to split wide open. There was a fireman eating breakfast in her kitchen and Mr. Campinelli was modelling a wedding dress for his wife. And there were feathers all over the floor, but she wasn't sure whether they'd come from a pillow or the huge white duck that was sleeping under her bed.

Nina slowly opened one eye and then the other, the disjointed dream dissolving in an instant. But the headache was still there, pressure at either temple. She slowly pushed up on her elbows until a wave of nausea made her stop. Through bleary eyes, she glanced at her surroundings. This wasn't her bedroom and she wasn't in her bed. And there wasn't an orchestra in her closet either.

It all came back to her, slowly. She was lying on Cameron Ryder's sofa, in her little black dress, with a hangover bad enough to lay low an entire fleet of hard-drinking sailors. Sucking in a deep breath, she tried to sit up again. This time she nearly made it to vertical before she was forced to stop.

From the meager light coming through the windows, she guessed it might be six, maybe six-thirty in the morning. For the first time in a long time, she'd slept the entire night through. Unfortunately, her dry mouth and tangled hair and aching head didn't make her feel completely refreshed. She felt as if she'd been run over by a city bus.

When she finally managed to get her feet on the floor, Nina noticed that she wasn't alone. At the foot of the sofa, Cameron had pulled up a chair. He lay sprawled in the soft cushions, his chest and feet bare, the top button of his jeans undone. Nina was afraid to breathe, afraid she'd wake him up. But he slept soundly, his hair mussed, his quiet expression boyish and vulnerable.

Though they hadn't spent the night in the same bed, Nina still felt a bit guilty. She should have left immediately, once she learned she wasn't at one of Charlotte's parties, but in Cameron Ryder's apartment. This whole plan to spy on him had been ridiculous, something she never should have let Charlotte talk her into! Good grief, she had no chance of resisting his charms— how could she possibly bend him to her will? She'd do best to gather her things, leave quietly before he woke up and turned that sexy smile on her.

On wobbly legs, she crawled off the sofa. "I need aspirin," she murmured. "I need water. I need a gallon of mouthwash." Nina took a quick look at Cameron, focussing on his mouth, the firm lips that had teased at hers, and that mussed hair that slipped so easily through her fingers. Drawing a ragged breath, she turned away, then wandered around the apartment looking for the bathroom. Two closet doors later, she found it through the bedroom.

She stared into the mirror above the sink. Her hair was a wreck and there were still dark circles beneath her eyes. She'd seen Charlotte come to the office looking exactly the same way and she wondered how the woman ever got any work done. Nina was tempted to turn around and crawl into the inviting comfort of Cameron's bed for another four or five hours of sleep.

She stuck her face under the faucet and gulped down a few mouthfuls of water, followed by a toothpaste chaser. She found the medicine cabinet behind the mirror at the end of the double vanity and didn't think twice before opening it, so desperate was she for aspirin. But as soon as her gaze took in the contents, she felt as if she were invading Cameron Ryder's privacy. Still, curiosity got the better of her.

Though she'd found very few personal items in his living room, there was no shortage of them here. She took out his razor and examined it closely, then drew it along her check. Her mind flashed an image of him shaving, fresh from the shower, a damp towel riding low on his hips. Then she imagined herself stripping the towel away and inviting him back into the shower with her.

Nina quickly set the razor back in the cabinet. His hairbrush came out next and she set it aside in favor of a bottle of his cologne. The moment she opened it, his scent drifted through the room. She dabbed a little on each wrist, pleased that she'd have a reminder of him for the rest of the day. But her next discovery was even more interesting—a box of condoms.

Nina reached for it, then drew her hand away. There were limits to her snooping. Had he bought the box recently, perhaps before the weekend they spent together in Maine? Or was the box nearly empty? She couldn't resist and tugged the box out of the cabinet. But it caught on the shelf bracket and when she yanked harder, the bracket flew off and the shelf dropped. As if in slow motion, it slid forward and then tipped and crashed onto the marble sinktop.

Bottles and tubes and razors and deodorant followed as a second shelf collapsed. Nina frantically tried to stop the avalanche of personal hygiene products but she couldn't. Scrambling to gather up the mess, she tried to avoid the broken glass. But when she reached up to the counter, a sliver embedded in the palm of her hand. "Ow!" she cried.

"What the hell is going on in here?"

Nina turned to find Cameron standing in the bathroom doorway, his eyes at half mast, his brow furrowed into a frown. He lazily rubbed his belly and yawned as he surveyed the scene of her latest disaster. She slowly got to her feet, then held up the box in her hand. "I was looking for..."

"Condoms?" he asked, his attention focussed on the box.

Just then, Nina realized what she was holding. She tossed it on the marble sinktop, as if it had burned her fingers. "No," she said. "Aspirin. I—I have a headache."

He bent forward and picked up a plastic bottle from the floor, then held it out to her. But when she reached for it, he frowned and pulled it away. "You're bleeding," he said, grabbing her hand.

Nina winced. "It's just a little cut. There's...broken glass."

Cameron shook his head, then gently pulled her out of the bathroom, taking care to steer her around the shattered shelf. "What is it with you and bathrooms?" he muttered.

Nina shrugged, too embarrassed to speak. She'd never had a problem with them before. Only since she'd met Cameron Ryder had she turned into one of the Three Stooges when she got around plumbing fixtures. "Just call me Moe," she said.

"Well, Moe, let's get that hand fixed." He showed her into the kitchen where he ran the cut under water. Peering closely at her palm, Cameron picked out the small sliver of glass, then dabbed at her hand with a damp paper towel. He kissed her wrist, allowing his lips to linger for a few seconds before pulling away. "Good as new," he murmured.

She leaned back on the edge of the granite countertop. "I'm sorry about the bathroom."

"Don't worry," he said, with a smile. "That bracket has been a little wobbly. I should have fixed it." He rinsed his hands then dried them off on a kitchen towel. As he set the towel down, her gaze caught his and they stared at each other for a long moment. Desire flared in his eyes, like a warm fire on a cold night, drawing her near. And then, as if a barrier between them crumbled, he reached out and took her face between his hands.

His mouth met hers and Nina wasn't surprised or shocked. The kiss felt like the most natural thing in the world. His tongue teased at the crease of her lips and she opened for him and drew deeply of his taste. She hadn't remembered this feeling so incredibly good. Every time he kissed her, she wondered why it always felt like the very first time. Her pulse quickened and she sank into his body, pressing her palms against his naked chest.

His skin, so smooth and warm, covered hard muscle. A light dusting of hair traced a line from his collarbone to his belly and she followed it with her fingers. When she splayed her fingers across his flat stomach, Cameron moaned softly. She hesitated for a second, but the moment of doubt and apprehension quickly fled beneath the warmth of his kiss.

When he grasped her waist and lifted her up to sit on the counter, Nina wrapped her arms around his neck, her gaze flitting over his face. He looked sleepy still, but his eyes were half-hooded not from exhaustion, but from need. He moved to stand between her legs and then, in one strong motion, he grabbed her hips and yanked her against him. His hand slipped beneath her thighs, and as he kissed her, he drew her legs around his waist, never breaking contact.

Nina knew she should call an end to this, that to go on would only complicate an already complicated situation. But it felt so good and she didn't want to stop. And at this very moment, she didn't care about Charlotte Danforth or *Attitudes* magazine or Cameron Ryder's plans to take it over. All she had on her mind was the wonderful way Cameron made her feel, with his lips, his tongue, his fingertips.

Her headache had miraculously disappeared, soothed by the rush of blood through her body. She felt dizzy and breathless, as if she'd suddenly found a way to fly without ever leaving the ground. Cameron's lips abandoned her mouth and moved to her neck and then her shoulder, tasting, nipping, sending delicious sensation to every nerve.

There was no way to refuse him, no chance to summon her resolve. The moment his lips touched her skin, Nina knew she was lost—and she didn't want to be found. Instead, she wanted to wander in this new world of overwhelming desire.

Cameron moved to the spot between her breasts, just above the neckline of her dress. He must hear my heart pounding in my chest, Nina mused. Her breath came in shallow gasps and she tipped her head back and furrowed her fingers through his hair. He lifted his head and looked directly into her eyes. They hadn't said a word to each other, yet he spoke to her with his every action and every caress.

She saw her reflection in his eyes and she was beautiful, seductive, powerful. The kind of woman who could drive him mad with need. At first, the depth of his passion startled her, but it didn't scare her. There was so much about Cameron Ryder that she didn't know, but what she did know was enough. Alone, together, their passion was undeniable. And deep inside, she also knew it was enduring. Cameron was no one-night stand. He was meant to be in her life forever.

With her legs around his waist, he grabbed her and picked her up as if she weighed nothing at all. As they moved from the kitchen to the bedroom, Nina nuzzled her face in the curve of his neck, his rough beard scratching her face.

With other men, she'd been nervous, apprehensive, but all Nina felt was excitement and anticipation. Since the moment they'd met, this had been coming. And though she'd only known Cameron for a short time, she was completely safe in his arms. She wanted him. She needed him. And most important, she loved him.

It didn't make sense, yet it made all the sense in the world. He'd been out there, in a city of three million people, waiting for her. And the moment she'd spilled coffee all over him was the very moment her life had turned a corner and headed down a brand-new road. Now there'd be another life-altering moment and Nina knew it was coming very soon.

He carried her into the bedroom and together they tumbled onto the bed, Cameron's weight warm and heavy on her body. He pushed up on his elbows and gently brushed the hair out of her eyes, dropping tender kisses on her lips. "Here we are again," he murmured, dipping down to steal another kiss.

His voice, ragged and deep and laced with desire, sent a shiver down her spine. "Here we are," she repeated.

"Nina, I want you to know that I—"

She pressed her finger to his lips. "Don't. No apologies, Cameron. Let's just start from here and forget about everything else."

He smiled crookedly. "Say that again. Say my name."

"Cameron," Nina said. "Your name is Cameron."

This time his kiss was swift and urgent, as if to seal this new beginning they'd found. He rolled Nina over on top of him, then slowly worked her zipper down from her nape to the small of her back. The dress was so form-fitting that she'd only managed a pair of panty hose beneath. His hands slipped beneath the open back and his fingers spread over her skin.

Nina sighed softly. The warm ridge of his desire pressed into her belly and she reached between them and touched him there. He sucked in a sharp breath the instant her hand closed over him, hard and ready beneath the fabric of his jeans. And then, it was as if another barrier had fallen between them and they began to frantically tug at each other's clothes.

As the sun brightened the windows of his bedroom, she gently sheathed him with a condom he'd retrieved from the mess in the bathroom. He braced himself above her and without taking his eyes from hers, Cameron probed at her damp entrance. And then, in a long moment of exquisite pleasure, he moved, slipping inside her so effortlessly it was as if he'd always belonged there.

Nina gave herself over to the delicious heat of him and the growing knot of desire that tightened with every stroke. Reality no longer existed, only this searing intimacy between them. And when her release was near, she called his name, first softly, then with more urgency.

He joined her at her peak, arching above her, his body tight, waiting for her. Then they tumbled down together in a rush of soft moans and tangled limbs, of frantic kisses and shattering sensation. And when her heart had finally slowed, Cameron wrapped her in his arms and she slept, deeply and without dreaming.

THEY SPENT MOST OF THE morning in bed, making love and then sleeping for a time, laughing and teasing each other until Nina was sure no other world existed except the one they'd created for themselves. She'd forgotten all about the pressure from Charlotte, the uncertainty of her professional future, and her doubts about Cameron.

When she finally pulled herself out of his arms and tried to get dressed for work, she could only think of the next time they'd be together.

"Come back to bed," he said. He lay on his side, watching her slip into the little black dress. The sheet, still twisted from their last bout of lovemaking, was draped over his narrow hips.

Though their lovemaking had been born of raw passion, fierce and undeniable, Nina still couldn't keep herself from feeling a bit guilty. She'd never gone to bed with a man quite so quickly and in broad daylight. By the calendar, they barely knew each other. But from the start there had been an unwavering connection and the knowledge that passion between them was inevitable.

"I can't," Nina said with a sleepy smile. "I have to get to work." It was the last thing she wanted to do, but she was anxious to talk to Charlotte. She was through with all this silly intrigue and if Charlotte didn't like that, she'd just have to cope. Nina wouldn't be stuck between them anymore, wouldn't pretend that she could ever betray her lover. A delicious shiver skittered up her spine. She liked the sound of that—her lover. "Zip me?"

Cameron crawled across the bed and got up on his knees, the sheet falling away to reveal a very naked and very aroused man. He turned her away from him, but rather than zip her dress, he wrapped his arms around her and began to kiss her back, working his way down her spine. "I like you much better without clothes." When he got to the small of her back, he pushed aside her dress and started toward her hip. "What's this?" he asked, his hand smoothing over her skin.

Nina glanced over his shoulder. "My tattoo?" A blush warmed her cheeks. In a moment of youthful enthusiasm, she'd gone along with a few of her artist friends and had the rose permanently colored on her body. "I know, it's a little—"

"I like it," Cameron said, nibbling at the spot with his teeth. "It's kind of sexy. I've never been with a woman who had a tattoo before." He turned her around. "Do you have any other tattoos or moles or scars you want to show me? I'm very interested in seeing them all."

Nina sighed and raked her fingers through his hair, staring into his eyes. She wondered about the other women in his life, whether he'd seduced them with such unabashed boyish charm. Had he loved any of them, even just a little bit? A tiny dagger of jealousy pierced her heart when she thought of him with other women. They seemed so perfect for each other it was hard to imagine that he'd ever been with anyone else.

She bent close and brushed a kiss across his lips. "It's nearly noon," she murmured. "Charlotte is going to wonder where I am." She'd probably be waiting for a report. Of course, she'd haul Nina out to a lunch of salads and martinis and by one o'clock, Nina's headache would return in full force. Maybe it would be better just to crawl back into bed with Cameron and show him the little heart-shaped mole on her inner thigh. She could face Charlotte and all her demands tomorrow.

No, she told herself, she should face Charlotte today! After what had happened between her and Cameron, any notion of her playing spy would have to end. She didn't want to be caught in between her boss and her lover anymore. "Cameron, I really need to go." She gently smoothed his tousled hair with her fingers. "Why don't you come over tonight for dinner? We'll spend a quiet evening. We'll talk." She pressed her forehead to his. "I'll even let you play with my trolls."

"Sounds like a deal."

"Seven?" she asked.

He nodded, but a moment later he cursed softly. "No, better make it eight. I've got to put in an appearance at a charity cocktail reception at Lincoln Center."

Nina waited for her invitation, sure it was going to come, yet determined to plead exhaustion and politely refuse. Besides, it was too early to make public appearances together. If Charlotte ever found out, there would be hell to pay, and Charlotte did have her spies all over the city, even if Nina wasn't one of them anymore.

They'd only just become lovers a few hours ago. Social obligations would have to come much later. But Nina couldn't help but imagine what it would be like to walk into a party on Cameron Ryder's arm. He exuded such quiet confidence, such pure masculine power, that every woman in the place would have to wonder how she'd managed to attract his devotion.

The truth was, she wondered herself. Maybe she would accept his invitation. She could wear one of the dresses that Charlotte had bought her and she'd ask Lizbeth for makeup advice. But the invitation didn't come.

"I'll have a quick glass of champagne and cut out early," Cameron said. He crawled out of bed and tugged the sheet along with him, wrapping it around his waist. "Let me make you breakfast before you leave."

Nina brushed aside her disappointment. Maybe it *was* a little too early for public appearances. She glanced around the room, searching for her shoes. Sheets and blankets and pillows were scattered everywhere, mute testament to their morning of lovemaking. With a soft sigh, she reached for a pair of his trousers, which had also ended up on the floor, and tried to restore the crease.

A smile curled the corners of her mouth as she smoothed her hands over the fabric. A strange warmth grew inside her as she took on the little task, such simple domesticity, almost intimate in nature. She wanted to believe they'd have a future together, that she'd be there to help him organize his life. But their future was still uncertain, and even though their lovemaking had strengthened their chances, she still felt riddled with insecurity.

As she shook the trousers out, his wallet slipped from the back pocket and landed on her foot. She quickly picked it up, then froze, fighting the temptation to open it and do a little more snooping. But this wouldn't be snooping for Charlotte. Nina wanted to know more about the man who'd made her ache with desire, the man who'd satisfied her need with such abandon. Glancing at the door to the bedroom, she quickly opened the wallet and flipped through the contents.

She giggled softly as her gaze fell on his driver's license. He had to be the only person in the state of New York who actually looked sexy in his license photo. After a cursory glance through his credit cards, she looked for photos, but oddly, he carried none—no old girlfriends, no family portraits, not even a favorite pet. A wrinkled piece of paper caught her eye and she pulled it out and unfolded it.

She blinked, her gaze immediately focussing on familiar handwriting. Her handwriting! "Looking for Mr. Right Now," she read. "Attractive, fun-loving, energetic SWF, 25, seeks adventurous Adonis, 25-35, for wild Saturday nights and lazy Sunday afternoons."

Her mind spun back to the night she'd written the ad, searching for a reason why he'd have it in his wallet. "The coffee," she murmured. She'd used the paper to wipe his shirt and then he'd snatched it from her hands. The implications of her discovery slowly sank in as her gaze took in the stationery the ad was written on. He'd known all along—her name, where she worked—from that very first night. And their "chance meeting" that second night was no accident at all. He came to the coffee shop looking for her. No, Nina corrected, he was looking for the woman who worked at *Attitudes!*

Nina cursed softly. And *she'd* been the one who'd been racked with guilt over her little spying assignment. How could she have been so naive, so stupidly trusting? A man who'd do anything for his business wouldn't think twice about using a woman for his own selfish motives. And she'd fallen right into his trap!

She refolded the wallet and shoved it back in his pocket, then tossed the trousers aside. Suddenly, everything had become so crystal clear, her mind spinning with newly discovered truths. No wonder he hadn't invited her to the cocktail reception! He probably had a date already, with some gorgeous, sophisticated socialite.

But as Nina stood in the bedroom, trying to work up a good case of anger, there was still a tiny shred of hope that she was wrong about Cameron's motives, that he'd kept the ad for other reasons—though, try as she might, she'd couldn't come up with one.

It all came back to one irrefutable fact—his stubborn refusal to give up his plan to take over *Attitudes*. A man like Cameron would do anything to make his business plans succeed, including seducing an innocent like herself. Although, after today, Nina couldn't really claim to be an innocent. She'd enjoyed their passions as much as he had—or pretended he had.

Nina glanced at her reflection in the mirror above the dresser, then combed her hair with her fingers. She hurried out to the living room, searching for her purse and tucking the paper inside when she found it near her shoes. She had almost made her escape when Cameron appeared and dragged her into the kitchen. He poured her a cup of coffee and handed her a piece of toast.

Nina bit into the bread, thankful to put something in her roiling stomach. "Maybe you should cook *me* dinner," she commented, attempting to keep the anger out of her voice. She fought the urge to confront him with her evidence, but she was so confused right now, she doubted that she'd be able to sort it all out in such a short time.

Cameron reached out and brushed a strand of hair from her eyes, the action causing her anger to subside for a moment. "What you see here is the extent of my culinary expertise," he said softly, taking the toast from her fingers and stealing a bite. "This and frozen TV dinners. Oh, and microwave popcorn. Maybe someday I'll give waffles or omelets a try." He grabbed her around her waist and put the toast back in her mouth. "Anything to keep you here in the morning."

Nina's breath caught in her throat as he kissed her neck. This was the perfect way to begin the day, even though, technically, the day had begun hours ago. Standing in the kitchen, sharing a piece of toast, she could almost imagine them living together, sharing every morning like this, and sharing every night the way they had in bed.

She tried to summon her anger again, to maintain her suspicions of him. But his eyes were so warm, his smile so genuine, she found her resolve faltering. "Do you have to work today?"

Cameron nodded. "Since I met you, work has been

piling up at the office. I should go in, at least for a little while."

"You should. After all, you have magazines to buy and lives to ruin." She'd meant the comment to be teasing, but it came out flat and accusatory, only serving to bring up a conflict that still stood between them. Nina's gaze dropped to the counter, guilt surging inside of her. "I'm sorry. I shouldn't have said that."

"Is this going to be a problem between us?"

She looked up at him. "I guess neither of us will know until it actually happens." Nina stood. "I'd better go."

He nodded reluctantly, then joined her as she walked to the door. She opened it, but he caught her before she had a chance to walk out. Cameron dropped a quick kiss across her lips. Nina knew if she didn't leave now, she'd never leave. She gave him a faint smile, then stepped out into the hallway.

"We'll talk about it at dinner tonight," he called as she got on the elevator.

"Dinner tonight," she murmured as the doors closed.

When she got to the lobby, she expected the doorman to hail a cab for her. But the same limo driver who'd brought her to Cameron's last night was waiting for her in front of the building this morning. She'd forgotten all about him. And she'd told him to wait for her. "You haven't been waiting all night, have you?"

He held the back door open and smiled. "Mr. Ryder called down last night and told me you'd be needing a ride this morning, Miss Forrester."

"He called you?" She frowned. Was he so certain

she'd stay, so confident of his seductive powers? "When was this?"

"Sometime after midnight. Where can I take you this morning?"

All right, so he hadn't been overly presumptuous. He'd called long after she'd fallen asleep, which could only be labelled considerate. Nina glanced at her watch, then at her parcels that were still sitting on the back seat. "Take me to Soho. Greene Street just north of Canal."

The driver nodded, then closed the door. As they started downtown, Nina shut the privacy screen. The tinted windows gave her perfect privacy as she wriggled out of her dress and began to rummage through the bags for something suitable to wear to work. She found a black skirt Charlotte had insisted was a crucial item in every woman's wardrobe and a sexy black sweater with a low-cut V-neck. She'd be forced to forgo the bra again and her panty hose were still somewhere in Cameron's bedroom. But she found a thong that would serve as the bottom half of her underwear.

She tugged it on, then winced. "Dental floss," she muttered, wriggling around until she was comfortable. When she was finally dressed, she grabbed a bottle of water from the refrigerator and sat back in the seat. Her mind wandered back to the ad that she'd hidden in her purse. What did it all mean? Had he somehow manipulated her for his own purposes? Had he used her without her even knowing? Or were her suspicions of him unfounded?

Brushing those thoughts aside, she focussed on the day ahead. She'd have to speak to Charlotte. She'd also have to fabricate an excuse for standing her up last night, completely forgetting the party she was supposed to attend the moment she stepped inside Cameron's apartment. And then there was her assignment as a spy.

She couldn't tell her boss about last night, not that there was anything to tell. The fact that Cameron used a twin-blade razor, wore designer cologne, and believed in safe sex wouldn't help her cause. And that he looked devastatingly sexy without clothes, had a little scar on his elbow and the cutest butt she'd ever seen was completely irrelevant.

Maybe she could make something up to get Charlotte off her case for a while, until she straightened everything out. She could confess she'd broken into his computer but he'd walked in and she'd had to stop. Or that she'd overheard him talking on the phone. She could probably come up with something that would satisfy her boss.

But what difference did it make? If Cameron wanted *Attitudes*, nothing would stand in his way, not even Charlotte's best attempts to save her magazine or Nina's attempts at espionage would make a bit of difference.

The limo pulled to a stop and Nina noticed they were just a half block from the headquarters for *Attitudes*. She lowered the privacy screen. "You can drop me off in the middle of the next block. The white cast-iron building just past the bus stop. And can you drop these bags at my apartment? Ring number one and ask Mr. Campinelli to hold on to them for me until I get home this evening."

"Certainly, Miss Forrester."

Nina hopped out of the limo before he could open her door. She glanced at her watch again. It was past one and Charlotte always left for lunch by one. If Nina was lucky, she'd avoid her boss for at least another few hours. That would give her plenty of time to get her thoughts in order.

"I am so weak," Nina muttered. "The man lies to me, not once but twice, and I don't even care. It's the sex. If it weren't for the sex, I could easily resist him. It has to be the sex."

She couldn't remember ever feeling such a powerful physical attraction before. There had been men in her past, some moderately interesting in bed. But she'd never once considered spending the rest of her life with one of them. They were musicians and artists and actors, not the kind of guys a girl could depend on. But Cameron Ryder was different. He was solid and dependable, exciting and dangerous. Nina sighed. If only she knew what he was really up to, whether he was truly interested in her or just in the magazine she worked for.

"Nina, darling!"

Nina glanced up to see Charlotte standing in front of the building. She groaned inwardly. Why now? She'd managed to limit her disasters to the immediate vicinity of a bathroom in the past twenty-four hours. But there was no bathroom in sight now. "Charlotte, I'm so sorry I'm late but—"

"Oh, never mind that. I'm sure you had a good reason. I was just going to lunch. Join me, won't you? And after that we can go shopping. I know of this extraordinary boutique in the Village that I just have to show you. They carry vintage purses and I know how much you love vintage." She looped her arm through Nina's. "And while we're shopping, we can discuss strategy."

Maybe she wouldn't have to confront her, Nina mused. She could make something up, toss Charlotte a few vague details to appease her, until Nina managed to work up the courage to quit her rather dubious career as an espionage agent.

"I did learn something interesting," Nina offered with a weak smile. "He has a very nice apartment on Riverside Drive."

7

"SO, CAM, who's the girl? Anyone I know?"

Cameron grabbed a glass of champagne from a passing waiter and took a quick gulp, then turned back to Jenna Myers, his business partner's wife. They stood near the edge of the crowd gathered in the opulent entrance hall to the Metropolitan Opera House, the Lincoln Center benefit a prelude to an opera opening.

The cause was a children's charity that was very important to him. What wasn't important was this silly gathering, everyone dressed in tuxedos and evening wear, simply to celebrate how much money they'd all contributed. But he'd agreed to attend the benefit reception with Jeff and Jenna Myers under one condition—that he could put in a quick appearance before catching a cab back downtown to Nina's place.

She'd promised to cook him dinner and he much preferred her company to that of the charity crowd. As he sipped his champagne, his mind wandered back to their morning in bed. Though he knew Nina was a passionate woman, he'd never expected that passion to be so completely uninhibited. Cam had never experienced such wild need with a woman before. Even now, hours later, it brought a flood of heat to his bloodstream.

"She must be special to make you smile like that," Jenna teased.

Cam blinked, then glanced down at her. "What?"

"The girl," she said. "Jeff told me about her." Jenna put on a pretty pout. "Though he was very short on details."

"What girl?" Cam asked with mock innocence.

"Don't be coy," she warned. "You're not good at it." She took a sip of her champagne. "Jeff says you've met a woman. And she's special. He said you took her away for the weekend."

"Special," Cam repeated. That was an understatement. Nina Forrester was more than special. She was fascinating and exciting and mercurial, the kind of woman he could spend a lifetime getting to know. Another image flashed in his mind—Nina lying back in his bed, her hair spread over his pillow, her eyes dazed with need. She'd been perfect, so soft and willing. Even now, with half a city between them, a rush of desire heated his blood and piqued his senses.

But the memories of their passions were now tempered with something else. He thought back to her wine-induced admission. *I'm a spy. Charlotte told me I have to be a spy to save the magazine.* The admission had bothered him all day long. Just how far was she willing to go to save her own job? He couldn't help but return to the ad she'd written. If she was willing to go that far to get a man, how far was she willing to go to save her job?

Cam wished he had a little more experience with women. Though he wanted to believe her motives were pure, he wasn't sure. In his mind, there was only one way to prove her true feelings and that was to go ahead with his business. If she really cared, then it would all work out in the end, her motives becoming irrelevant. "Yeah," he finally murmured. "She's special."

"Then why didn't you bring her tonight? I'd love to meet the girl who turned my favorite geek into the Casanova of the computer world."

Cam shook his head. "I couldn't bring her," he said. "Things are still a little complicated between us."

"Are you in love with her?" Jenna asked, in that same direct way she always spoke to Cameron.

Cam never had any doubt why Jeff had married her. In the past, he'd wondered whether he'd find someone as beautiful and kind to spend the rest of his life with. "Yeah," he said. "Maybe. Probably. But it's not that simple."

Jenna nodded. "Ah, the magazine. Jeff told me about that, too. I've read *Attitudes*. It's kind of fun. A little bit out there, but fun. It would be a nice match for NightRyder."

Cam glanced at his watch. He'd been at the reception for precisely one hour. He reached out and grabbed Jenna's elbow. "I really have to go. When Jeff gets back from working the room, tell him I promised the foundation another twenty thousand for next year. But no publicity and no photos, all right?"

Jenna nodded, then pushed up on her toes and pressed a kiss to his cheek. "She better know how lucky she is to have you." With an apologetic smile, she wiped the lipstick away. "We wouldn't want her thinking you've been with another woman, would we?"

Cam chuckled. "No, that wouldn't be so good."

"Bring her along next time," Jenna said. "I'd love to meet her."

"I will," Cam said. With that, he started toward the door. Along the way, he met several business acquaintances and stopped for a moment to chat. But his mind was firmly fixed on the tiny apartment in the East Village and the woman who waited for him there. He managed to avoid a group of photographers stationed near the bar and then picked up his pace toward the exit when he came upon a woman he'd dated several years ago.

She smiled at him as he passed, then stepped toward him. Anna Lowell. But Cameron gave her a quick wave and kept walking. Odd, how his standard of true feminine beauty had changed. He used to believe Anna was stunning. He supposed she still was. She was long-legged and raven-haired, a sultry beauty who turned heads whenever she walked into a room. He'd been proud to have her on his arm—the geek and his gorgeous date.

But she did nothing for him now. A petite blonde now held the standard, mischievous blue eyes and honey-blond hair, slender limbs and a tiny waist. But there was more to Nina than just beautiful looks. There was the sound of her voice and the lilt of her laughter, the twinkle in her eyes when she teased him. And there was the passion and the need, the soft moans and the gentle sighs, the amazing sensation of moving inside of her.

He turned to take a last look around the room, happy to see that Jeff had made his way back to Jenna's side. But as he started toward the door, the sight of another woman caught his eye. He glanced to his side and, for a moment, Cam was certain he'd seen Nina— or maybe her double.

In just a few fleeting seconds, he recognized the way she moved, the exact color of her hair, her shapely legs and lithe body. Cam took a few steps in her direction, wondering what she was doing here. But as the woman disappeared into the crowd, he stopped, then shook his head.

"You really must be in love," he murmured. "You're seeing Nina Forrester everywhere you go."

Cam turned on his heel and started toward the door. The real Nina was waiting for him at her apartment and, right now, he didn't want to imagine the blue of her eyes or the silken feel of her skin. He wanted to experience it firsthand.

NINA RISKED A LOOK over her shoulder just as she reached the safety of the ladies' room. She pushed the door closed behind her and only then began to breathe again.

"This was a mistake," she muttered. "Whatever possessed me to follow him here?"

When the idea first occurred to her, after an agonizing lunch with Charlotte, she'd merely been curious. Was he coming to the reception alone? And why hadn't he at least made an attempt at inviting her? As the afternoon wore on, her suspicions about Cameron

Ryder seemed to grow by degrees, plaguing her brain until she was desperate to know the truth.

Nina had convinced herself that if she saw him with another woman, then it would be over. She could finally put an end to all the confusion and the insecurity. So she'd put on another slinky little dress that Charlotte had bought her and grabbed a cab to Lincoln Center. She hadn't had a plan, but figured no one would question her presence, as long as she looked as if she belonged.

Standing at the entrance, she had searched the cavernous foyer for Cameron and had just caught sight of him when an elderly gentleman approached and asked for her invitation. Her attention still fixed on Cameron, she was amazed at how gorgeous he looked in a tux. The fine tailoring and black color made him look so sexy and more than a little dangerous. But her brief journey into fantasy ended when the gentleman insisted on seeing her invitation.

Luckily, Nina had had the presence of mind to drop Charlotte's name, claiming that she'd been asked to attend the reception in her boss's place. After checking his list, the explanation seemed to satisfy the man and he left her alone. But the moment she turned back to look for Cameron again, her gaze fell on the evidence she'd been dreading.

It was then she noticed the beautiful woman who stood next to him, her hand resting on Cameron's arm. His head was bent close, as if everything she said was of such import that he didn't want to miss a word. A tiny flare of jealousy grew to a flame and she didn't move, transfixed by the sight of Cameron Ryder and the other woman.

She was so beautiful, dressed in an expensive gown, slender, dark-haired, oozing sophistication. And when she pushed up on her toes and playfully placed a kiss on his cheek, Nina's heart twisted. She hadn't wanted to be right, but the proof had been standing just twenty feet away!

Nina had taken a step back, ready to leave. But at that very moment, Cameron had glanced around the room and, for a brief instant, their gazes met—at least she thought they had. That's when she'd made her escape to the bathroom. And that's where she was right now, hiding, ashamed and upset by what she'd done and seen.

Nina hurried over to the sink and stared at her reflection in the mirror. She wasn't sure what she expected. Maybe she hoped that she didn't really look like herself. That maybe, sometime during the cab ride over, she'd magically transformed into Julia Roberts or Madonna or someone that didn't look a bit like Nina Forrester. But no, there she was, the same woman she'd looked at in the mirror every day of her adult life.

"Maybe he didn't really see me," she said. "Maybe I just think he did."

Nina sighed, then ran her fingers through her hair. What difference did it really make? She had the ad she'd found in his wallet. She'd seen the other woman with her very own eyes. What more did she need to prove that Cameron Ryder was a scoundrel and a snake, a manipulative bastard with a heart of stone?

The door to the bathroom opened and a few

moments later another woman joined Nina at the mirror. She glanced over and her breath froze in her throat. It was her! The other woman! Nina swallowed hard and forced a polite smile as she nodded.

"It's getting so hot out there," the other woman said, fanning her face.

She had a pleasant voice and a friendly smile and Nina immediately sensed that she wasn't the trampy slut she'd assumed she was. In truth, she looked really nice and not nearly as sophisticated as she had from across the room. "I—I know," Nina murmured. "And noisy. I just had to come in here for a little quiet." She drew a shaky breath. "Don't you just hate these receptions?"

The woman smiled. "Oh, not really. It's my husband who hates them," she said.

"Your—your husband?" Oh, God. Nina felt faint and nauseated and dizzy all at once. Cameron Ryder was married? How could she possibly have missed that? Sure, he kept a low profile, but nothing in his behavior had suggested that he had a wife hiding at home. She looked at her reflection again and noticed that all the color had drained out of her face. Or maybe he wasn't married and he was having an affair with a married woman. That was almost as bad.

The woman nodded. "I had to practically drag him here. After a hard day at work, he just wants to stay home and relax. But I love to get dressed up and go out. After spending my day with two kids, a little excitement is just what I need."

"Kids? You have kids?" Oh, this was even worse!

She nodded as she reached into her purse. Nina watched as she expertly applied her lipstick, then dabbed it off with a tissue. "What does your husband do?"

"He works for NightRyder. It's a dot-com that's very—"

"Oh, I know NightRyder," Nina said in a dull voice.

"Jeff and his college buddy, Cameron Ryder, started the company when they were students. Just a couple of computer nerds and now look where they are. Hobnobbing with New York's social elite." She held out her hand. "I'm Jenna Myers, by the way. I don't think we've ever met."

"Jeff?"

"He's my husband," Jenna said, giving Nina an odd look. "I'm Jenna. Jenna Myers."

A flood of relief washed through Nina. "Oh, Jeff," she said, a smile breaking across her face and the color returning to her cheeks. "And Jenna. Jeff and Jenna." She took Jenna's hand. "It's a pleasure to know you both. And your children. I—I'm Nina. Nina Forrester."

Her face was warm and she tried to hide her relief. So Cameron hadn't been with another woman. He'd come alone and met Jeff and Jenna here. And of course, he and Jenna were friends. This was all so innocent. Nina could see now that Jenna was an easy person to like. Nina already liked her. "So you must know Cameron Ryder pretty well. What's he like?" Nina sensed she could trust the opinion of Jenna Myers. If she said he was a scoundrel, then he probably was.

Jenna dropped her lipstick back in her purse and snapped it shut. "He's the most eligible bachelor in

New York City, but no one knows about him. He's an absolute hermit when it comes to the media. But then, that's probably for the better. He might not be a bachelor for much longer."

Nina's joy automatically dissolved. "No?"

Jenna shook her head. "He's met a woman and I do believe he's head over heels in love with her. I don't know much about her, just that he's having dinner with her tonight. He couldn't find the door fast enough once he put in his appearance."

A tiny thrill raced through Nina. Jenna was talking about her! Cameron was having dinner with her. But the thrill didn't last long. "Cameron left?" Nina asked.

Jenna frowned. "A few minutes ago. Why?"

Nina backpedalled. "I was hoping to get a chance to meet him. I—I just love NightRyder." She swallowed hard. "I should really be going too. I have an early day at work tomorrow." She sent Jenna Myers a quick smile. "It was nice to meet you, Jenna. Maybe we'll meet again sometime soon." Jenna opened her mouth, no doubt to end their conversation with a pleasantry, but Nina was already out the door.

She pushed her way through the crowd at the coat check and nervously waited as the attendant retrieved her wrap. If she could catch a fast cab back to her apartment, she might make it there before he did. If he stopped at his apartment to change first, she'd actually have a good chance of slipping in without him ever knowing she'd followed him here.

Nina hurried out to the street and tried to hail a cab. She luckily got one as another pair of guests pulled up for the reception. She hopped inside. "The East Village," she said. "And if you get me there fast, I'll give you a very big tip."

The driver nodded and screeched off, honking his horn at another cab as he pulled out into traffic. Nina nervously clutched the edge of the seat as they sped through traffic, running yellow lights and changing lanes in the blink of an eye. A tiny smile fought through the immediate fear of a cab accident. Maybe Cameron didn't have any ulterior motives. Maybe she'd been wrong about him.

What had Jenna said? She searched her mind for the exact words. *He's met a woman and I do believe he's head over heels in love with her.* Nina wanted to believe that what she'd said wasn't an exaggeration, or a simple way to warn off all interested single women. Could Cameron actually be in love with her?

It was all happening so quickly. People didn't fall in love after just a week! That only happened in the movies and in romance novels and in schoolgirl dreams. No, the most she'd allow herself to believe was that Cameron had a sincere affection for her, and a passion, and need so strong that neither one of them could deny it.

When they pulled up to the apartment, Nina slumped down in her seat and peered out the window. There he was, sitting on her front stoop, still dressed in his tuxedo. Nina moaned softly. "Can you drive around the block?" she asked the cab driver. She could sneak in the back, change, then claim she was in the shower. After all, he was a few minutes early.

She paid the cabbie double, then took the back stairs two at a time. When she got inside her apartment, she kicked off her shoes, tossed her wrap and purse under her bed and ripped her dress and underwear off, hiding her clothes in her closet. She grabbed her robe and wrapped it around her naked body, then raced to the bathroom and stuck her head under the faucet. When her hair was sufficiently wet, she twisted it in a towel then headed to her intercom.

She pushed the button and spoke into it. "Cameron? Are you out there?"

A few seconds later, he replied. "Nina? I didn't think you were home."

"I was in the shower when you rang. Come on up." She buzzed him up, then opened the front door. Her heart was still hammering from her sprint up the stairs. Nina pressed her palm to her chest and tried to slow her heart. It had almost resumed its normal speed when Cameron appeared on the stairs. She felt it skip, then start hammering again. He looked so sexy in that tux, she mused as a smile curled her lips. So sexy she was tempted to rip it off and have her way with him.

"Hi," she murmured, leaning up against the door-jamb.

"Hi," he replied. "You look pretty."

"And you look handsome." A faint blush colored her cheeks as she fiddled with the towel. Their eyes met. "I—I'm sorry to make you wait. I was in the—" Suddenly, she couldn't think.

"Shower?" he asked.

Nina nodded, then stepped aside and let him in. "Dinner is nearly ready," she lied as she closed the door. "I hope you like lasagna." She pointed to the sofa and calculated how long it would take to thaw the frozen entree sitting in her freezer. "Why don't you sit down?"

Cam did as he was told, sinking into the cushions and draping his arms over the back. "How was work? Did you get into trouble for being late this morning?" He grinned. "Or was it afternoon?"

"No trouble. Charlotte's a little preoccupied with her own concerns." She hesitated, wanting to say more, but then didn't. She was tired of thinking about Charlotte and her precarious position at work. Cameron was here and he looked so incredibly delicious. She didn't even want to think about dinner.

Cameron sighed. "Nina, you don't have to worry about what you say to me. It's not going to make a difference. I know everything I need to know. Charlotte is putting together a financing package to bring the magazine into the black. Her father is pushing her to sell. Ad pages have dropped nearly fifteen percent in the past six months. And the IRS is looking to audit her previous two years' tax returns. A little problem with deductible business expenses, I understand."

Nina gasped. "How do you know all this?"

"I have my spies," he teased. "The same as Charlotte probably does."

Her eyes went wide and she blinked. "Spies?" She tried to disguise her distress with a bland expression.

"My financial guys have lots of connections," he continued. "So, I probably know more about Charlotte Danforth than you do." He patted the cushion beside him. "I don't want to go over this all again. Come on, sit down. Dinner can wait."

She sat down next to him and folded her hands on her lap. "I just wish this wasn't happening," she said. "It just confuses things even more."

Cam reached out and softly stroked the hair at her temple, tucking a tendril behind her ear. "It shouldn't make a difference," he said.

"But it does. You should be the enemy. I should hate you or at least want to see you fail. But I can't do that. Whenever you're near, I just want to..."

"You want to what?" He wrapped his arm around her shoulder and pulled her against him. He nuzzled her neck. "Do you want to punch me? Slap me? Make me pay for all my sins?"

Nina shook her head, his teasing lightening her mood. "No."

He pulled back and tipped her chin up until she looked into his eyes. "Maybe you want to kiss me?" he asked, brushing his lips over hers. He took her hand and placed it on his chest. "Or touch me?" he continued, grazing her jawline with his mouth.

When he reached her neck, she sighed softly. "We should really talk about this," she said.

He chuckled softly. "Maybe we're not using words, but I'd definitely say we're communicating, aren't we?"

He pushed her back into the soft pillows of the sofa, Nina knowing full well they'd have to face their differences sooner or later. But for now, she was content to lose herself in the heady taste of his kisses and the soft caress of his hands. As they slowly tugged at each other's clothes, she let her thoughts drift, enjoying the flood of sensations that raced through her body.

It didn't make a difference, she reassured herself as he pushed aside her robe and nuzzled the warm flesh of her breast. Nothing made a difference but this, she thought as he moved inside of her. All that really mattered were these incredible feelings between them. As long as they had passion, what more did they need?

"I'M GOING TO QUIT. That's my only way out of this mess."

Nina glanced over at Lizbeth. Her friend was stretched out on a chaise with a tin-foil reflector bathing her face in the sun's rays, the neckline of her dress pulled down low, the hem hiked up high. The warm spring day had brought them both up to the roof of the *Attitudes* building during their lunch hour and to Nina's relief they were alone. She'd been waiting all day to talk to her friend.

Lizbeth raised her brow but didn't open her eyes. "Quit? What are you going to do for rent? For food? If I see you begging in the subway, I'm not going to give you money."

Nina shrugged. "I'll go back to waitressing, or dog grooming. Or I could find a whole new career. I just can't take this pressure anymore. Charlotte is making me nuts and I think I'm getting an ulcer."

"Honey, you can't quit. If you quit, then you'll be poor and, sooner or later, you'll want to stay on my couch. And my couch is Italian leather and it's really not meant for people to sleep on. Besides, there's no guarantee you'll have a future with this guy if you do quit. Is he going to pay your bills? Before long, you'll be out of a job and out of a man. And that's just about the worst thing that could happened to a girl...except for premature wrinkling."

"Don't you see?" Nina answered defensively. "This is the only way out. If I stay, Charlotte will drive me insane until this whole thing is over. And who knows when that will be? And if she finds out I haven't been spying for her, then she'll fire me anyway. Either way, I'm out of a job."

"You could always dump him," Lizbeth said. "Get rid of him and keep the job."

The notion of dumping Cameron had never even occurred to her. "If I dump him, Charlotte will fire me anyway. I'm still out of a job."

"Then get him to dump you. Charlotte can't fire you for that. Pick a fight and get him angry enough to stop calling for a few weeks. Then, later, after this all settles down, you can apologize or he can apologize. If he really loves you, he'll be back. And making up is so much fun."

Lizbeth's words echoed in Nina's head. *If he really loves you. If he really loves you.* Maybe she could get him to dump her or at least make the attempt. It would be a good test of his feelings for her. Maybe if she put it all on the line, she'd finally figure out how deep the connection really was.

"That's not a bad idea," Nina said. "I could always push my feelings about the magazine. You know, give him an ultimatum. But he claims that *Attitudes* is business and I'm...pleasure. He has the ability to separate the two, unlike me. All I know is that I'm really tired of pretending to be Pussy Galore. I've been making up things to tell Charlotte just so she won't get suspicious."

In the pantheon of Bond femme fatales, she'd been a complete failure. Though she had managed to lure her man into bed not once but twice, and the sex had been pretty incredible even by Hollywood standards, she couldn't bring herself to betray him. Her stomach fluttered as images of the previous night flashed through her mind—the feel of his skin against hers, the ragged sound of his breathing close to her ear, and the delicious sensation of Cameron moving inside of her, arching above her as he reached his release.

She was usually so pragmatic when it came to sexual matters. But with Cameron, she couldn't be near him without wanting him. When she wasn't with him, their time together constantly rewound in her head until she was nearly frantic to see him again. She'd tried to convince herself that her feelings were nothing more than infatuation, just that wonderful rush of hormones that fades after time. But if this was infatuation, then she didn't even want to consider what loving Cameron Ryder might be like.

"Tell him you want a commitment," Lizbeth suggested. "Mention the 'C' word and most men will run like a cheap pair of panty hose."

Nina considered the proposal. With most men, it might just work. But if Jenna Myers really spoke the truth, then any mention of long-term monogamy was pretty risky. He might just agree and then where would she be? Nina frowned and shook her head. Isn't that what she should want—a happily-ever-after? And if it was, why was she contemplating picking a fight with him? Oh, this was all just way too confusing. "I'm not so sure that will work either, not since last night."

Lizbeth turned to her, this time squinting at Nina. "Last night?" Her gaze turned shrewd. "Nina...what happened?"

Nina drew a shaky breath. "We got a little carried away and we—"

"You didn't!" Lizbeth cried, sitting up and tossing her sun reflector aside. She dropped her designer sunglasses down from the top of her head and snatched up her Diet Coke, wriggling in her chaise until she was comfortable. "Tell all."

"Three times, maybe four last night. And I lost count yesterday morning," Nina admitted. "In fact, I might have lost consciousness, too." She sighed. "I've had more sex in twenty-four hours than I've had in the past year. Maybe even two years if you consider quality as well as quantity."

Saying it aloud suddenly made it so real. Yet, it still seemed like a dream. It had happened in such a short time, just a week and a day since that night in the coffee shop when she'd met "Jack Wright."

"Did you tell Charlotte?" Lizbeth asked.

Nina gasped. "Of course not!" Besides, what would she tell Charlotte about such intimate matters? Nina could reveal that Cameron Ryder had an incredible body and that the touch of his hands on her naked skin sent waves of pleasure racing through her, and that making love to him had been everything she'd imagined it might be. But she preferred to keep those opinions to herself.

"But if she knew you actually seduced her mortal

enemy, she'd make you editor-in-chief. This is what she wanted, this is why she put you on the job. Sex is above and beyond the call of duty. She just wanted a little inside info and you got some real...inside info."

"I wasn't thinking about duty," Nina said. "Besides, I didn't seduce him on purpose. He seduced me. Though I liked it...a lot."

"You're not actually falling for him, are you?" Lizbeth asked, watching Nina expression for a hint of her true feelings.

Nina shook her head, then slowly stopped. Why lie? If anyone could offer advice, Lizbeth could. She reluctantly bobbed her head up and down. "How can I be in love with him? We've only known each other a week, and a day."

Lizbeth laughed. "You've never heard of a little thing called love at first sight? Honey, that's the only way to fall in love. It saves so much time and effort."

"That only happens in the movies. And it wasn't love at first sight. When I first met him, I didn't think he was my type. And then there was that whole coffee fiasco. I'd call it mortification at first sight for me, and irritation for him."

"So, what do you want? Do you want him to dump you or to marry you?"

"I don't know," Nina said with a sigh. "I just want a way out, a way to get Charlotte off my back. I'm stuck in the middle and, no matter how this mess turns out, I'm afraid I'm going to lose—either the job or the man, or maybe both."

"If you're really in love with him, then I don't have to ask which one you want to keep."

Nina didn't want to say it out loud for it wasn't exactly the most professional thing in the world. She'd worked so hard to get this job; it had always been her dream to work in publishing. And the thought that she'd give it all up for a man was just too much to admit. Her parents would probably disown her and her feminist friends would refuse to speak to her. She had bills and obligations! And she couldn't bear to go back to working odd jobs, and with the publishing business so tight, who knew when she'd be able to find another position with a magazine?

The last thing she wanted to do was move back home with her mom and dad. Life on Long Island was sheer torture. "I don't know what I'm going to do. I'm just so confused."

Lizbeth tipped her glasses back up and returned to sunning her face with the reflector. "You could always introduce him to your friends. They'd scare anyone off. Or better yet, start dating Dagger again. Jealousy could cause a man to walk away, at least for a little while." She smiled. "In fact, I've often found jealousy to be a wonderful way to pique a man's desire. You just let Dagger steal you away from Ryder, then let Ryder steal you back." She opened one eye and turned to Nina. "On second thought, it's a powerful weapon and shouldn't be used by amateurs. I wouldn't recommend it for you. It could be dangerous."

Nina considered the notion for a moment. It would be a way to figure out where she stood with Cameron. If she could make him jealous, then he might be so angry, he'd leave her alone for a while. And once everything was settled and his anger had cooled, they could start again. And Dagger would be perfect. He was so different from Cameron, what man wouldn't be left feeling inadequate?

Dagger—also known as David Wells—was an artist from London. They'd met while she was working at a restaurant and he was living on bottomless cups of coffee and cigarettes. He had fit right in to her existing group of friends—painters, musicians, students, bohemians, all penniless but captivated with life in the city. He was crazy and sweet and incredibly talented, and definitely not the kind of guy a girl could depend on.

"Dagger has a gallery opening tomorrow night," Nina said. "I got the invitation a few weeks ago. I suppose I could…"

"I'm warning you, honey, be careful. The last time I saw Dagger, he had purple hair and wore eye makeup. The man is crazy. Cameron Ryder might not get jealous, he might just take off running in the opposite direction."

"Dagger doesn't have purple hair anymore," Nina said. "It's bleached blond. I ran into him last month. And he quit with the makeup. He actually looks pretty normal except for the earrings. Besides, the hair and makeup were an artistic statement."

"And the name?"

"You never liked him, did you?" Nina lay back and closed her eyes, tipping her face to the warmth of the sun. They sat in silence for a long time, before she sighed softly. "Maybe I will take Cameron to the opening."

So she finally had a plan, Nina mused. It was a nice

little test. If he passed, then she'd achieve two of her objectives—she'd get Charlotte off her back and she'd figure out how Cameron really felt about her. And if he really loved her, then a little fight wouldn't keep them apart for long. She'd just tell him that she couldn't see him until all the business with the magazine was settled.

She could always do that without the whole jealousy test, but Nina was willing to risk it. It was time for her to force his hand, to decide where she belonged in his life. Which was more important to him in the end—her or his business? If he truly loved her, as Jenna Myers had claimed, then she should be the most important thing in his life.

And like Lizbeth said, making up was so much fun. A tiny shiver skittered down her spine and suddenly she felt cold. She was taking such a risk with a relationship that was still so tenuous and so new. But she had to make something happen, something had to change or she'd be caught between Charlotte and Cameron until she was the one who paid the dearest price.

Right now, the only person she could trust to make decisions about her life and career was Nina Forrester. And even if her own heart betrayed her at every turn, if her feelings for Cameron led her to heartache, she would be the one to determine her future.

8

CAMERON STARED at the crowd gathered on the street outside the Wilton Gallery in TriBeCa. Unlike the society crowd at the Lincoln Center benefit, this group was more...colorful. When Nina had suggested the gallery opening, he'd jumped at the chance. The opportunity to meet her friends hadn't been offered before and he was more than a little curious. If he was to have a real future with Nina, he wanted to know everything about her. Meeting her friends would be an important first step.

"Maybe we shouldn't go in," Nina murmured, clutching his hand. "It seems pretty crowded."

He gave her a sideways glance. She looked particularly pretty tonight, wearing a body-hugging, sequined T-shirt and black satin pants that rode low on her hips and revealed a tantalizing view of her belly button. A bright pink furry jacket topped off the ensemble. Cameron had come right from work and wore his usual suit, causing any number of stares as they walked down the street together.

"I want to go," Cameron said. "We've done things that I wanted to do, now we should do something you want to do. That's what dating is all about."

"Is that what we're doing?" Nina asked. "Dating? I—I mean, do you consider yourself my boyfriend?"

Cameron thought about his answer for a long moment. "Yeah, maybe. We skipped the preliminaries, but there's no reason we can't go back and get them right, is there?" He moved to cross the street, but Nina held him back.

"These people really aren't your type," she said. "And the art is very *avant-garde*. That means weird."

He slipped his arm around her shoulder and gave her a playful hug. "I know what *avant-garde* means, Nina. And I like all kinds of art. Who knows? I might even find something I want to buy."

Though she forced a smile, her expression told him that she wasn't really happy. She looked nervous, like she was about to bolt. "Are you worried what I might think of your friends? Or are you worried what your friends might think of me?"

Nina shrugged. "I—I'm not worried."

"We could always go home and I could change into my leather pants and studded vest."

A gasp slipped from her lips. "You have leather pants?"

He chuckled and kissed the top of her head. "No, but if you think they're crucial to our relationship, I'd be happy to buy a pair. Now, are you ready to go? I want to see what this Dagger is all about."

Nina smiled and for the first time since he'd picked her up, she seemed to relax. "Are you sure you don't want to go back to my place? We could have some wine, watch a video and maybe..." She left the rest up to his imagination.

Certainly the potential of having hot, passionate sex was more interesting to him than a gallery opening, but they'd have plenty of nights together. He tugged on her arm and she stumbled off the curb after him. "How do you know this Dagger guy?"

"We're old friends," Nina said wanly.

Cam stared down at her, trying to read her feelings. Old friends? Had they dated? Had she once loved him? He cursed silently. So many unanswered questions only pointed out the obvious—he really didn't know Nina at all. He knew the feel of her skin beneath his hands and the sound of her breathing when she slept, but he knew nothing of her past, her family, her dreams. Maybe this night would give him a few more answers.

"Just promise me that if you're having a bad time, we can leave," she said, hurrying to keep up with him.

When they reached the gallery entrance, he dropped a quick kiss on her mouth and grinned. "Promise." He pulled the wide glass door of the gallery open and waited as Nina stepped inside and handed the attendant the invitation. He followed, but then stopped short. The gallery was packed with people, all of them dressed as outrageously as Nina. Music throbbed from the sound system and cigarette smoke drifted through the air. Dagger drew a very flamboyant crowd and Cameron was willing to bet that he was the only one in attendance who didn't have any tattoos or piercings.

For some unknown reason, he suddenly imagined all these people at his wedding—to Nina. Though he'd thought a lot about their future, he'd never actually pictured their wedding before. But now, as he glanced around the room, he could only imagine what an interesting day that might be. He shook his head, brushing aside the image.

"See," Nina said. "This really isn't your scene."

"Not so," Cameron said. "This is what NightRyder is all about. Though we usually stick with concerts and night clubs, gallery openings look like a good bet." He stepped behind her and rested his hands on her shoulders. "Can I take your jacket?"

She shook her head, drawing it more tightly around her. "Actually, I'm a little cold," Nina murmured. "And we're going to be leaving soon, so I'll just keep it."

"I'll go get us something to drink," Cameron said.

He slowly pushed his way through the crowd, wondering why Nina had brought him in the first place. She seemed determined to leave before they'd even stepped inside. Could she be ashamed of him? The thought brought a soft curse to his lips. They weren't exactly a perfect match, at least not on the surface. But then Cameron wasn't really the man he pretended to be either. He was really a jeans and T-shirt kind of guy, not just a man in a designer suit. The suit was only for effect, to give him more power and credibility in his business dealings.

As he looked around the gallery at the guests, he felt a certain kinship to most of them. They'd probably been teased in high school, maybe even spent a few hours shut inside their lockers too. There wasn't that much difference between the freaks and the geeks. But Nina didn't know that. She'd probably always been popular, although he wasn't sure of that either.

Though they knew each other intimately, they didn't really know each other at all.

The bar was set up at the rear of the gallery and he grabbed two white wines and started back toward Nina. But just as he caught sight of her over the crowd, he watched as a man pulled her into his arms and kissed her full on the mouth. Frowning, Cam hurriedly pushed through the people blocking his way until he stood beside them both. He expected her to notice him there, but she was so lost in the kiss, her arms wrapped around the guy's neck, that a bomb could go off beside her and she wouldn't jump.

Like half the other men at the party, the guy was dressed in black, wore at least three earrings, and sported a bleached blonde crewcut. Cam waited for a long moment as they continued kissing before he shifted both glasses of wine to one hand and tapped the guy on the shoulder.

The guy drew away and sent Cameron an impatient glare. In truth, Cam was tempted to punch the guy in the nose, but that wouldn't cause the best first impression among Nina's friends. He'd never in his life felt such a surge of raw jealousy, but he drew a deep breath and held his temper. "That's my date you're kissing," Cam said.

"Oh, yeah?" He looked at Nina. "This guy's your date, Neens?" He gave Cameron the once-over, taking in the conservative suit, then chuckled. "Where'd you find him? Wall Street?"

With a wan smile, Nina shook her head. "Dagger, this is Cameron Ryder. Cameron, this is the artist known as Dagger."

Dagger immediately let go of Nina and she stumbled backwards. Cam grabbed her elbow to steady her, then handed her a glass of wine which she promptly gulped down. She watched the interplay between them with wide eyes. Dagger held out his hand and Cameron reluctantly took it. "It's a pleasure to meet you, Dagger," Cam said.

The guy's pierced eyebrow quirked up. "Cameron Ryder? You wouldn't be the Cameron Ryder who runs NightRyder?"

Cam nodded. "I am."

The artist brought his hands to his head and pressed them against his temples in disbelief. "Oh, man. Neens, you didn't tell me the stuffed shirt you were dating was *the* Cameron Ryder. I *love* NightRyder. Listen, man, I think the Internet is the next big canvas. I want to paint in world colors, international brush strokes, you know what I mean? We need to talk, I mean, really talk. We could do some things together, bring my art to the masses."

Cam nodded, not sure at all what Dagger meant, but willing to give him the benefit of the doubt. All he really wanted to do was draw Nina into a dark corner and kiss away any memory she had of the man. He nodded again then reached in his jacket pocket and produced a business card. "Call me at my office sometime next week and we'll set up a meeting."

Dagger stared at the card. "Wow, man. Cool. Cameron Ryder. Who would have thought?" He turned and wandered off into the crowd, his attention still focussed on the business card, not even bothering to say goodbye to Nina.

"That's Dagger," Nina murmured as she strolled along a wall of paintings, sipping her wine. "You made his day."

Cameron chuckled and placed his hand on the small of her back as they moved through a crowd. "No, I think you made his day. I take it you're more than just friends?"

"We used to be more," she explained with a ragged sigh. "Maybe we still are," she added, under her breath. She stopped in front of a large painting and stared at it, but Cameron could only watch the play of emotion across her face. "What do you think of this one?" she murmured, the color high in her cheeks, her eyes bright.

He glanced up at it, then turned his attention back to her, curious at her strange mood. What did she mean, maybe they still were more than just friends? "Very nice."

"It is," she said. "It's one of his best works. He really is quite talented."

Her attention was so fixated on the painting that, this time, Cam looked at it with a greater eye to detail. It was a female nude, reclining, long-limbed and slender and—Cam frowned. There was something about the image, something familiar.

His gaze stopped on a tiny section of the painting, a rose placed on the hip of the model. He stepped closer and examined it. With a gasp, he looked back up at the face of the figure, the golden blond hair draped over one breast, the playful smile. "This is you," Cam said, astonished by what he saw.

"Now can we go?"

He perused the painting for a long moment, speechless, not from the fact that the woman he was with was on the canvas, naked, for all to see, but because the artist had captured her so perfectly. He saw the Nina he'd fallen in love with—the tantalizing mix of girl and woman, the vulnerability and the determination, and beneath it all, the hint of the unexpected.

Cam had purchased a number of pieces for the NightRyder headquarters, so he knew something about modern art. And he knew he liked this painting, though it wouldn't adorn his office. This was a painting meant for the bedroom—his bedroom. "It's beautiful," he murmured.

"You—you like it?" she asked, her tone laced with skepticism.

"How much is it?" he countered.

Nina gasped. "You're not going to buy it, are you?"

He shrugged. "Why not? That's what it's here for, isn't it?"

"But—but you can't. You know it's me. You can't buy this."

"It's beautiful," he said. "As beautiful as you are."

"I forbid you to buy this painting!" Nina said, stomping her foot. She glanced around, then dropped her empty wineglass on a passing tray. "I'm leaving. You can come if you want or you can stay here, but I'm leaving. This night was a huge mistake." With that, she turned and worked her way through the crowd.

Cam watched her head toward the door. Somehow, he was missing something here. He thought she'd brought him to the opening so he could meet her friends, but it almost seemed that she was more interested in pricking his temper than introducing him to acquaintances. She'd been on edge all evening, though he'd done nothing to make her angry.

He followed her, but just as he got to the door, Dagger caught him, anxious to introduce him to a group of his artist friends. Cam listened to a few moments of their conversation, then held up his hand. "Listen, I have to go." He reached in his pocket, withdrew his wallet, and grabbed most of the cash he had inside. "I want the big painting over on the far wall. You know the one." He slapped the cash in Dagger's hand and closed his fingers over it. "This should be enough. I'll stop by tomorrow to pay the balance and pick it up."

He left Dagger with his mouth hanging open and his friends showering him with congratulations. Though he had much more important matters to tend to, he didn't want anyone else buying that painting.

The painting was his and Nina was his. Unfortunately, convincing a seven-by-seven foot piece of art to come home with him was a lot easier than convincing Nina Forrester to do the same.

NINA WAS TRYING to hail a cab, when Cameron came out of the art gallery. He scanned the street and she tried to shrink behind a small tree. But he caught sight of her almost immediately and hurried over.

This whole evening had been a disaster. She'd brought him here hoping to pick a fight. She'd kissed Dagger, flaunted a nude painting of herself, and run out on him and all he'd managed to do was insinuate himself into her life even further. He'd made friends with her old boyfriend, he'd shrugged off the painting as if she were showing him a picture of a bowl of apples, and he'd actually looked like he was enjoying himself in a place where he had no chance of fitting in.

Nina shot a glance over her shoulder and waved more frantically for a cab. But every cab just flew right by, leaving her to face Cameron and his questions. He stood beside her on the curb and for a long time didn't say a word.

When he finally spoke, his voice was calm. "Would you like to tell me why you're so angry?"

She fought the urge to turn on him, to grab his lapels and give him a good shake. Why did he have to be so wonderful, so incredibly romantic and alarmingly obtuse? "Because you're supposed to be jealous and you're not. And because you wanted to buy that stupid painting even though it cost three thousand dollars. And you were supposed to hate Dagger. Instead, you're his new best friend."

Her reasoning took him completely off guard, a fact that pleased her no end. "He's your friend, Nina. I thought you'd want me to like him."

"If you were a real guy, you would have punched him when you found him kissing me. But you're not a real guy. You're some paragon of manhood, some white knight, some guy I can't help but fall for."

Cameron frowned. "Let me get this straight. You want me to be angry? And jealous of Dagger?"

"He's a nice guy. He's good looking. And we used to be lovers. And he saw me naked—a lot more times than you did, bucko. And—and that tattoo you're so fond of? Well, he was there when I got it!"

Cameron grinned, a smile that only piqued her

irritation with him. "Nina, we both have people in our pasts. But they don't matter. Besides, he doesn't get to see you naked anymore, does he?"

"No," she said.

"And I do."

Her eyes narrowed. "You did. Past tense." She turned on her heel and started off down the sidewalk. Maybe she could catch a cab on the next block.

"Well, not exactly," he called in a teasing tone. "I bought the painting."

Nina screamed in frustration and continued to walk, cursing to herself with every step.

"All right, all right. Would it make you happy if I admitted I was jealous? That when I saw Dagger kissing you I wanted to throw him against a wall and punch his lights out."

"I don't believe you," she shouted over her shoulder. "You're just saying that to make me feel better. Besides, it's too late. You're never going to want to dump me now."

He hurried to catch up to her, then grabbed her arm and spun her around. "What the hell are you talking about? Why would I want to dump you?"

"Because I can't do this anymore," Nina blurted out, tears pressing at the corners of her eyes. "I'm tired of being stuck between you and Charlotte. Tired of trying to figure out who's using me and why. Do you know she's had me spying on you? I'm supposed to report back to her with anything I learn about your business. And I have no doubt that everything I say to you is ending up in some business file somewhere."

"I knew," he said.

"Knew what?"

"About the spying. You talk in your sleep. You mentioned it the other night at my place. Nina, you don't have to be stuck in the middle. Nothing you do is going to stop this from happening. And nothing you say is going to make a difference. Why can't you just accept that?"

"Why?" she repeated. "Because this job means something to me."

His jaw went tight. "Hell, Charlotte can't even remember your name. You have a tiny little office with no windows. And they probably don't pay you half of what you're really worth."

"Welcome to the real world, Cameron Ryder," she said, her voice cold. "Things may have come easily to you, but they didn't come easily to me. Do you know what I was doing a few years ago? I was cutting poodles' toenails at a dog grooming salon. And before that, I worked for a cab company, cleaning the insides of cabs. You wouldn't believe what goes on inside cabs. And I was a bicycle messenger for three days until I fell off my bike and gave myself a concussion. And in between all those jobs, I schlepped corned-beef sandwiches and potato salad in a deli. And then, I got my foot in the door at *Attitudes*, a national publication, and I started to dream that I might just have a career—until you came along."

"Why does your dream have to change? You'll still have a job after I buy the magazine."

"But it won't be a job that I got because I'm good. It'll be a job you're letting me keep because I'm sleeping with you."

"You want me to fire you?"

"I want a job in editorial," she said.

"Then you want me to promote you."

Nina clenched her fists. "No! You don't understand. I don't want you at all. I just want you to leave me alone."

He took her hands, but she pulled away. "Nina, I don't think you have any idea what you really want."

"Maybe I don't. But I do know one thing. I wish I'd never met you. I wish I'd never spilled that coffee on you."

A cab screeched to a halt right in front of her and Nina grabbed the door. But Cameron put his hand over hers. "Let it go."

"I want to go home," she said, trying to keep her voice even. Her frustration mixed with the stark realization that she'd fallen in love with Cameron Ryder and there was nothing she could do about it. They'd known each other a week and she was ready to throw her fate into his hands, to trust him with her professional dreams as well as her personal desires.

What did she really know about him besides what she'd experienced in the bedroom? He was completely inflexible about *Attitudes*. Would that same inflexibility slowly seep into their relationship until all she'd have left were regrets? Though her heart told her to love him, she just couldn't believe it was all so simple.

"Please," she said. "I just need to go. Let me go." She pulled the door open and hopped inside. To her relief, he didn't follow her. As the cab pulled away, she closed her eyes. If she could just put some distance between them, just take some time to regain her perspective, maybe her life wouldn't seem like such a big mess.

Nina twisted and looked out the back window, but the gallery was already a block away and any chance to see him again was gone. She turned around and settled herself in the broad back seat. All she needed was time. She'd get over Cameron Ryder, if she just put her mind to it. And in a few weeks, her life would all be back to normal, just as if she'd never met him.

THE EVENING WASN'T GOING nearly as well as Cameron had hoped. He sat across the table from Nina and watched as she flipped through her menu, her expression cool, her gaze distant. After their argument in front of the gallery, Cam had decided to give her a little time to think. He hadn't called her or tried to contact her for three days. And then it had taken him another four days to convince her to meet him for dinner.

When she'd first walked into the restaurant, he'd fought the urge to yank her into his arms and kiss her senseless. He'd thought about her every minute of every day and it had been sheer torture not seeing her. But there were too many things standing between them, too many outside influences pulling them apart, for them to even carry on a rational conversation.

Nina dropped the menu on the table and placed her hands in her lap. She looked uneasy, as if she'd rather be any place than sitting across from him at one of New York's best restaurants. He'd tried to engage her in idle conversation, but she'd have none of it, barely commenting on the menu choices and clamming up completely when he asked if she was hungry.

When the waiter arrived, they managed to order. The young man had noted the strained silence between them and quickly fetched their salads, then made himself scarce. By that time, Cameron had had enough of her cool mood. "Did something happen at work today?" he asked. "Not that I'm interested in any inside information. I'm just concerned. You seem a little stressed out."

Nina sent him a suspicious look. "Nothing much. Charlotte is still upset and she's picked me as the shoulder she prefers to cry on, even though I told her you dumped me." She stabbed a piece of lettuce, a little more enthusiastically than necessary, then popped it in her mouth. "Oh, there was something that came up," she said, almost offhandedly. "There's a picture circulating around the office that might interest you."

Cameron glanced up from his own salad. "A picture? You work at a magazine. I suspect there are a lot of pictures in your office that would interest me."

"This is a picture of you," Nina explained, her gaze fixed on his. "It was taken by a freelance photographer who works for *Attitudes*."

She was watching for his reaction. Cameron had worked hard to protect his privacy. The thought that he'd let down his guard, even just once, caused a tiny sliver of aggravation. "I don't remember having my picture taken."

"Yes, I know. You usually avoid photographers. And now I understand why."

Cameron had learned from past experience that it was best just to get whatever was bothering her right out in the open. Allowing Nina's temper to simmer only resulted in an overblown reaction to circumstances that were usually very minor, a trait he found both charming and exasperating. "I take it there's something about this photo that bothers you?" he asked.

"No," Nina said, setting down her fork. "But it will probably bother you. It's a picture of you and another woman kissing, at that Lincoln Center reception that you went to the other night."

He blinked. "I wasn't with another woman—except for Jenna Myers. She's the wife of my business partner."

"That doesn't make any difference to Charlotte. She's going to use that photo against you. She's going to publish it and tell everyone about your little affair. She'll turn it into a scandal. She's running an article on the 'Internet's Hottest Bachelors.' I'm already working on the research."

"She thinks Jenna and I are having an affair?" Cameron asked. "Well, you can tell her the truth. Jenna is a friend and there's nothing between us."

Nina shook her head. "I'm afraid I can't do that. After all, that photo is business. And you're...well, you know how important it is to separate the two. That's one of those unbreakable rules you live by, isn't it?"

He toyed with his fork, twisting it around and around in his fingers. "You and I have a relationship, Nina, whether you're willing to admit it or not. And you know the truth about that photo. There's nothing between me and Jenna. If you really care about me, you'll convince Charlotte not to use the photo."

Nina cursed beneath her breath. "And if you really cared about me, you'd walk away from *Attitudes!*"

"That's a completely different thing."

"Not to me."

Cameron set down his fork and reached out to take her hand, but she evaded his grasp. He sighed in frustration. "Nina, I've only had a few girlfriends in my very limited social life. Hell, you know what I looked like in high school and that pretty much held for college as well. I wasn't exactly fighting them off. I've never really had a serious relationship. I've dated, but I've never cared about anyone the way I care about you. You have to understand that I'd never do anything to hurt you. Trust me."

She stared at him a long moment, as if trying to decide whether to believe him or not. "Trust you," she repeated softly. "The only person I can really trust is myself." She leaned down and grabbed her purse from the floor. She withdrew a paper, unfolded it and tossed it in his direction.

Cameron picked it up and glanced at it. He recognized it immediately. It was the copy of the ad that he'd taken from her that first night. "Where did you get this?"

"I took it from your wallet. I was snooping," she said. "Or maybe you could call it spying. But then, that was business."

He tossed the paper back on the table. "And you're angry that I kept this? Hell, Nina, you're the one who gave it to me."

"And you're the one who pretended that you didn't know who I was that second night. You came back there to meet me, to use me in your big plan to take over *Attitudes*."

"I did come back there to meet you, but only because I was intrigued. Isn't that why you came back a second time? Besides, what difference does it make whether I figured out who you were the first night or the second night? It doesn't change anything."

"It's your intentions that make me suspicious," she countered.

Cameron smiled. "Nina, I've always made my intentions regarding you perfectly clear."

Nina quickly stood and threw her napkin on the table. She grabbed her purse, then stalked off in the direction of the ladies' room, leaving Cameron to contemplate his next move. He already knew how he felt about Nina Forrester. As far as he was concerned, she was the woman he wanted to spend his life loving. And if his instincts were right about Nina, she loved him too.

He tossed his napkin on the table and followed her to the bathroom. Taking a quick look around the foyer of the restaurant, he carefully pushed the door open and stepped inside. To his relief the bathroom was empty. He bent down and peered under the stalls. Only Nina's shoes were visible. Cameron leaned back against the door and flipped the lock.

He strolled to the mirror, then ran his fingers through his hair. Flipping on the faucet, he washed his hands and was just finishing when she emerged from the stall. She stopped short when she saw him, her hands frozen at the waistband of her skirt. Cam watched her reflection in the mirror, her eyes wary, her lips pressed into a stubborn line.

Then she slowly shook her head and stepped up to the sink. "Charlotte is going to publish the photo, you know. Whether it's in *Attitudes* or another magazine, it's going to be made public. She'll be sure of that. And nothing I say will stop her."

Cameron turned and rested his hip against the sink. "You could tell her the truth."

"And you could put an end to all of this if you'd just drop your offer to buy *Attitudes*. It's simple. If you cared about me, you'd let it go."

"And if you cared about me, you'd realize that it doesn't make a difference." Cameron fingered the small velvet box in his pants pocket. He'd bought the ring yesterday, determined to make her see how much he wanted her, how much they belonged together. "I think you know that, Nina, but you're putting the magazine between us on purpose. You don't have to side with anyone. This isn't your fight."

"It's my job," she said, stepping around him and starting toward the door, "and my life."

Cameron cursed softly. "No, Nina, I'm your life. And once you realize that, a job isn't going to stand between us." He slowly reached out to touch her, but she avoided his caress. "Don't think this is some game I'm playing. This was never meant to hurt you. It's business and sometimes business can get a little messy."

"That's a feeble excuse for what you're doing," she said as she grabbed the doorknob. She gave it a tug, but the door didn't open. Then with a frustrated sigh, she flipped the lock. But it still wouldn't open. Nina stepped aside. "I want to leave. Would you please unlock the door?"

"Not until we're done talking," he said.

"I'm done and I want to leave. Now open the damn door!"

Cameron reached for the lock, but no matter which way he turned it, it refused to open. "I think it's stuck," he said, pleased that he and Nina would be locked in the bathroom for a while. If this was what it took to solve their problems, then maybe the broken door was fate.

A panicked expression froze on her face. "No," she said, pounding on the door. "This is not happening to me again."

"You and bathrooms," he said with a shrug. "I should have figured something like this would happen."

"This is not my fault." She pounded a little harder. "Hello! Help! The door is stuck. Can anyone hear me?"

A few moments later, a muffled voice answered. "Hello? Is there a problem?"

"Who am I talking to?" Nina asked, pressing her forehead against the door.

"This is the manager," he replied. "Who is this?"

"We're stuck," Nina called. "He locked the door and now it won't open."

"He? There's a man inside there with you?"

"Yes. Call the fire department. Or a locksmith. You have to get us out of here."

"I think we have a key around here somewhere, ma'am," the manager said. "Please remain calm. We'll have you out in just a few minutes."

Nina turned, then closed her eyes and leaned back against the door. Cam fought the urge to reach out and touch her face, to run his finger along her lower lip, to weave his fingers through her hair. He thought about the first time they made love, how he'd carried her to the bedroom, her legs wrapped around his waist.

"Nina, I want you to know that since I met you, you've been the most important thing in my life. You're the only woman I've ever wanted to spend every minute of every day with. You have to believe me."

She opened her eyes. "It doesn't make any difference," she said softly.

"It makes a difference to me." He took a step closer, determined to kiss her. But when he bent his head, she stepped to the side, slipping away from him. "I have to get out of here."

"Nina, they'll get us out. Until they do, we should talk about this. We can fix this. I know we can."

She shook her head. "You could lift me up to that window," she suggested.

Willing to do anything to make her happy, he walked over to the window. "It's too high," he said. "You'll break your leg dropping to the ground outside."

"Just lift me up," she ordered. "After I'm out, I'll get a ladder and you can climb out."

He bent down and laced his fingers together. She kicked off her shoes, then put her foot into his hands. He took a moment to admire her leg, the sweet curve of her calf and the delicate shape of her foot. His fingers instinctively cupped her ankle and he fought the urge to unlace his fingers and run his palms along the length of her leg.

"I'm ready," she said with an edge of impatience.

"If the drop is too far, you have to come back down," he said. "I don't want you getting hurt."

"Just boost me up there."

Cam did as he was told. "It's probably got bars on the outside. You'll never be able to open it."

Nina unlocked the window and swung it open, then wriggled halfway out the window. "It's all right," she said. "There's a drainpipe I can hold on to." A few seconds later, her hips were through the window, then her feet. When she reached the ground, he heard her call out again.

"Toss my shoes through the window," she called.

Cam took aim and both pumps flew through the open window. He waited for a few seconds, waited for some acknowledgement from her. "Nina? Are you still out there?"

"I've thought about this for a long time and I have only one thing to say to you, Cameron Ryder. If you really care about me, then you'll walk away from *Attitudes* magazine. If you can't do that, then I never want to see you again."

"You're not going to get a ladder, are you," Cam said.

But she didn't answer. She was already gone. He pressed his hands against the wall and stared up at the open window. Nina Forrester was getting harder and harder to hold on to. If he didn't do something soon, she'd disappear from his life altogether. And Cameron knew he didn't want that.

With a soft curse, he slid down and settled himself on the cold tile floor. He'd be out soon enough. When he did get out, he was going to make sure that they settled things between them once and for all. He had no intention of taking the ring in his pocket back to Tiffany's, not matter how stubborn she tried to be.

9

"Is Charlotte in?" Nina stalked toward the elevator, not listening for Kathy's answer. She impatiently punched the button, waiting for the doors to open. "Call up to her office and tell her I have to see her immediately," she shouted as she stepped inside.

Nina had had all night to think about her situation and she'd made a decision. Cameron Ryder knew how she felt and now it was time to let Charlotte know exactly where she stood. "I'm not going to take this anymore," Nina muttered, watching the numbers above the door light up with each floor that passed.

When the doors opened again, she headed straight for Charlotte's office, ignoring her assistant's plea to stop. Nina flung the door open, then realized why Charlotte had requested her privacy.

"Nina! Good morning. Isn't it a glorious day?" Nina's boss lay stretched out on a table, a strategically placed towel the only thing standing between her and her birthday suit. "Hans, this is Nina. She works for me. Nina, this is Hans, my masseur. He has the best hands in Manhattan."

"I—I'm sorry," Nina murmured. "I can come back later."

"Don't be silly," Charlotte said, rolling over and sitting up. She tucked the towel around her body, then hopped off the table. "Same time next week, Hans?"

The masseur gave Charlotte a peck on the cheek, then walked out of the office. When he'd closed the door behind him, Charlotte sighed, then flopped down into her huge leather chair. She reached for a cigarette. "I've been so tense lately, but now, everything is just fine."

"The massage helped?"

"No. I got a call first thing this morning from Cameron Ryder." She sent Nina a sly smile. "He's coming in at ten to talk business. And considering the little surprise I have for him, I don't think he'll be coming back for a second meeting. I think we've saved *Attitudes* from the sharks."

"The photo," Nina murmured.

"I assume you told him about the photo," Charlotte said after taking a quick puff of her cigarette. "I certainly didn't say anything."

"Of course I told him," Nina said. She paused. "But then you knew I would. You were counting on it."

"Yes, I was. He's a charming man, Nina. Irresistible, perhaps. And those eyes—one look into those eyes and I'd tell him all my secrets, too. But now I have the upper hand. Once he realizes I'm ready to expose his affair, he'll back off and find some other magazine to buy."

"I wouldn't count on that," Nina said. "When I told him you planned to use the photo against him, he didn't seem to be concerned. He's still determined to buy *Attitudes*, regardless of your threats."

"It sounds so sordid, doesn't it? Like extortion or

blackmail. But then, I prefer to think of it as…hardball. When you play with the big boys, you have to play by their rules. Besides, I'm not the one who threatened him. You did."

"I did your dirty work," Nina said, Charlotte's motives becoming crystal clear. "No one can accuse you of blackmail now."

"So, what did he say? Tell me everything."

Nina shook her head and forced a smile. "The woman in the photo is the wife of his business partner."

Charlotte clapped her hands together. "Oh, how juicy," she said.

"There's nothing between them." Nina sighed. Now was the time to put an end to it. She was sick of playing Charlotte's little game. "If you publish that photo and say differently, he could sue the magazine. If I were you, I'd take his offer. You know he has the money and the power to make this happen. Maybe it would be best to just—"

"Give up?" Charlotte asked, stunned by the notion.

"I'm just offering my opinion. You don't know Cameron Ryder. He gets what he wants."

Charlotte leaned back in her chair and took a long puff of her cigarette, all the while keeping her gaze fixed on Nina. "Well, I can see which side your bread is buttered on, Nina," she snapped, stubbing out her cigarette in a nearby ashtray.

"My bread? You think I've taken money from him?"

"I have no idea how far you've gone to betray me. I only know that you're fired," she said.

Her words were short and direct, the statement

taking Nina by surprise, yet not really surprising her at all. She'd been expecting it since the moment she'd agreed to spy for Charlotte. "I've done everything you asked," she said. "You wanted the truth and I gave it to you. It's not my fault you don't like what I have to say. Besides, you can't fire me, because I came in here to quit."

"Well, I fired you first," Charlotte said, adjusting the towel as she stood. "You can collect your things from your desk. We'll mail you your last paycheck. And don't expect a letter of recommendation. An employee who doesn't show absolute loyalty to me and the magazine has no place here."

Nina pushed to her feet and stalked to the door. "I quit," she repeated.

"You're fired!" Charlotte countered. "Now, move along. I have a busy day ahead of me and no time to chat." But she paused before she pulled the office door open. "Before you go, let me offer a bit of advice. To Cameron Ryder, his business is the most important thing in his life. And even though you're in love with him, he couldn't possibly love you. A man like him isn't capable of love."

"I'm not in love with him," Nina said, knowing the words were a lie, yet hoping they might someday be true.

Charlotte clucked her tongue. "Come now, Nina. It's written all over your face. You want him to have this magazine. That way, you think you'll be able to call the shots." She shook her head. "You're a fool to believe in him. He's not interested in you. It's always been about the magazine, can't you see that?" She pulled her office door open. "This magazine is mine and it will remain mine. Your feelings for him make you a liability and I can't tolerate liabilities." She waved her hand, as if to shoo Nina out the door. "Go ahead, gather your things and say goodbye to your friends."

Nina hurried back to her office, then closed the door behind her. Tears of frustration threatened to spill from the corners of her eyes, but she held them back, focussing instead on her anger. "How dare she?" Nina muttered. "I did everything she asked."

Perhaps she'd been doomed to fail from the start. After all, how could she possibly ignore her feelings for Cameron Ryder? From the moment she'd met him, she'd felt an undeniable attraction, a desire unmatched by anything she'd ever felt for a man before. Yet he hadn't loved her enough to give up his plans for the magazine. There was no way she could have won and she should have seen that from the start.

Nina circled her desk and grabbed a shopping bag from the bottom drawer. "Fine," she murmured. "I'll go. Let's just see how this magazine gets along without me. No one works harder than I do. No one!" She grabbed her things from the top of her desk and dropped them in the bag. Within minutes, she'd taken everything she wanted. Her card file went in the bag last. It had taken her nine months to collect all the names and numbers of experts in every field. She wasn't about to give it all to her successor, the poor thing.

When she was finished, she took one last look around her tiny office then drew a shaky breath. Oddly enough, she'd probably miss the place. She'd certainly miss the security of a paycheck every two weeks. "I can always go back to waitressing," she murmured, "or dog grooming." Or maybe, if she was lucky, she could find a position as a fact checker with another magazine.

Nina peeked out the door before stepping into the hallway. If she could just make it to the elevator without seeing anyone, she might be able to salvage a small measure of her pride. She tossed her jacket over her shoulders then said a little prayer as she headed to the elevators. When the doors opened, she hurried inside.

As they closed, Nina leaned back against the wall and drew a long breath. She should feel more upset, more angry. But, in truth, all she could feel was pure relief. There'd be no more games, no more worries. Though she didn't have a job, she had marketable talents and a nice Rolodex. "There are other jobs out there," she murmured. "And I'm going to find them."

And there were other men as well. But Charlotte's words came back to her, ringing in her ears like an echo. Yes, there were other men. But none that she loved as much as she loved Cameron Ryder.

The doors to the elevator slid open and she stepped out. But she wasn't watching where she was going and ran right into someone else. Her bag nearly slipped from her fingers and she just barely caught it before she glanced up.

"Nina!"

For a moment, her voice had deserted her. She looked up into familiar green eyes and swallowed convulsively. "Cameron. What are you doing here?"

"I have a meeting with Charlotte Danforth." He glanced down at the bag she carried. "What's this?"

"My things," she murmured. "Charlotte just fired me. Or I quit, depending on whose version of the story you believe."

Cameron gasped. "What?"

"Oh, don't worry," Nina said with forced gaiety. "I'm not upset at all. In fact, I'm relieved. Now I won't be stuck in the middle anymore. I can turn my energies into finding another dead-end job at another struggling magazine with another crazy boss. And I can waste another year hoping for an editorial job that I'll never get. And I can thank you for that."

He reached out and took her hand, but she yanked it away from him. In truth, she wanted him to pull her into his arms and wrap her in his embrace, to soothe the ache in her heart and tell her he'd make everything better. "Nina, this was never meant to hurt you."

"Well, it did. And it will hurt plenty of other people, too. But then, it's business, isn't it."

"I can make this right," he offered. "I want to make it right."

She hefted the bag up into her arms. "Don't bother. I'm past caring. I'm just glad it's over and I can get on with my life." With that, Nina turned on her heel and walked out. This was all for the better, she told herself, trying to ignore the tears that burned at her eyes.

After all, she'd known him for two weeks. Nina Forrester didn't fall in love in fourteen days. No one did. And Cameron Ryder was never meant to be Mr. Right. He was Mr. Right Now for a few days and that was all. The sooner she realized the truth of that, the sooner she could put him in the past.

But as she walked out the front doors of *Attitudes*,

she knew that putting Cameron Ryder in the past would be an impossible task. Every man that came after him would always be held up against him, measured against the way he made her feel. Nina suspected they'd all pale in comparison. Even though she'd never see him again, he'd still be in her life and in her dreams. And though that fact should have made her heart ache, Nina didn't care. The ache would only remind her that she'd made the right decision.

"I'VE DECIDED not to buy *Attitudes*," Cameron said. His announcement echoed through the silent conference room, as did the soft gasps that followed.

"What?" The word came in unison from both Jeff Myers and Charlotte Danforth. Charlotte's attorneys and financial advisors took the news with startling stoicism.

"You heard me," Cam said. "I don't want the magazine. I'm withdrawing our offer."

Jeff reached out and placed his hand on his arm, as if Cam had suddenly lost his mind. "I really think we should—"

Cam shook his head, silencing Jeff's concerns. He hadn't really intended to give it all up, not until he'd seen Nina in the hall, looking so vulnerable, so forlorn. Hell, he should have given it up a long time ago, the minute he set eyes on her. But he'd been too stupid to realize what it was doing to them. Too stubborn to give up something he'd wanted for such a long time.

But there was something else he wanted more. Nina Forrester. And if it took giving up every penny he had, every nickel he'd earned, he was willing to do it. Nina was his life, not work, not business deals and Internet acquisitions. They belonged together and he was going to make that happen—starting now.

Charlotte glanced at her advisors. "Can he do this?"

"Of course I can." Cameron reached out and grabbed the contracts from Jeff, then started to rip them in half. But he stopped and set them down in front of him. "I do have one condition though."

Charlotte crossed her arms and set her chin stubbornly. "And what is that? You want the negatives of the pictures, I presume."

"That, too," Cam replied. "I also want you to give Nina Forrester her job back. In fact, I want you to give her that job she wanted in editorial. And for as long as she's employed by this magazine, I'll make no move to buy you out."

Charlotte shifted uneasily in her chair, her gaze darting between Cam and her attorneys. "I fired her this morning. She might not want to come back."

"I'm sure you can make it worth her while," he said with a smile. "An apology and a substantial raise should do the trick. Oh, and the promotion, of course."

"And what if she decides to quit later?" Charlotte asked. "I don't want you coming around in a year or two."

"Then it would be in your best interests to keep her happy." He glanced down at the contracts he held. "Very happy. Do we have a deal?"

Her advisors whispered into each ear and Charlotte nodded. "Deal."

With that assurance, Cam ripped the contracts in half and tossed the pieces on the table. Then he pushed back from the table and stood. "I can't say it's been a pleasure doing business with you, Ms. Danforth. But I hope that you work out your financial problems. For Nina's sake, if not for yours. I trust you'll call her today with the news?"

Charlotte nodded again.

Satisfied, Cam grabbed his briefcase and walked out of the conference room, Jeff Myers hard on his heels. His partner didn't say a word as they walked to the elevator, didn't say anything as they rode down to the lobby. But the moment they stepped out onto the street he turned to Cameron, a look of disbelief suffusing his expression.

"What the hell was that all about?" he asked.

Cameron shrugged. "I changed my mind."

"We've put months into this acquisition. It's been part of our strategic plan for the past three years and you just threw it all away. Is this about that woman? That Nina girl?"

"Nina Forrester," Cameron murmured, savoring the sound of her name on his lips. "And yes, it is."

The look of disbelief on Jeff's face slowly dissolved into a smile. "You're really in love with her, aren't you."

"I am," Cam admitted.

"You've never been one to mix business with your personal life."

"Maybe that's because I never had a personal life," Cameron said. "And now I do. And I don't want to ruin it over some stupid magazine. Hell, we've got the resources to start our own magazine. If Charlotte Danforth can do it, so can we." He stepped to the curb and hailed a cab, ignoring the limo that waited a half block away. "When you get back to our office, get our people started on it right away."

"You realize you've only known her for a couple weeks don't you?" Jeff asked.

Cam nodded. "Yeah. But I know how I feel. The first time I saw her, I knew she was the one. It wasn't until I saw her again that I was completely sure. And after that, it was easy. I guess love at first sight isn't so far-fetched."

Jeff clapped his hand over Cam's shoulder. "I guess not. So what are you going to do?"

"I'm not sure. I figure I'll wait for a few days, until she gets settled in her new job. Then maybe I'll pay a visit to that coffee shop across the street. After all, that's where it started."

"You've got it bad for this girl." Jeff laughed. "I'm glad. It's about time you had someone special in your life."

A cab pulled up alongside the curb and Cam reached for the door. "I'll be back in the office later today."

"Where are you going?"

He looked at the cab, thought for a moment, then shrugged. "I'm not sure. Someplace quiet where I can think." He drew a deep breath of the crisp spring air. "I've got to figure out how to get her back. And considering how I feel about her, I've got to make that happen soon."

"IT'S JUST A DATE," Nina murmured to herself. "It's just a date. No strings, no pressure. Just a date."

Though she'd been chanting that mantra since she'd walked out of the office ten minutes before, the words hadn't calmed her down. Maybe she ought to chant "It's just a job" instead. After all, that's what it really was, this meeting she'd set up with a complete stranger, a potential Mr. Right Now.

Her ad had been placed on the Personal Touch page last week, given a prominent position near the top of the column as requested by Lizbeth. After all, this was her first story assignment as the newest editorial assistant for *Attitudes* magazine and she was going to make sure it was a great story.

Looking for Mr. Right Now. Attractive, fun-loving, energetic SWF, 25, seeks adventurous Adonis, 25-35, for wild Saturday nights and lazy Sunday afternoons.

Just as Lizbeth had predicted, the ad drew a huge response. She and Lizbeth had poured over the three hundred letters and chosen five potential dates, five guys who claimed they were definite Adonises. Charlotte had insisted she meet at least five different men in order to provide a nice cross-section of the type of male reader who responded to their ads. She'd also reluctantly agreed to let Nina do a sidebar on the four marriages resulting from ads placed in the Personal Touch column.

The names ticked off in her mind. Lana Martina and Greg Healey. Brooke Weathers and Chase Davenport. Tyler Sheridan and Nick Romano. And Jane Dobson and Charles Warren. Four perfect love stories. They'd all found each other through the pages of *Attitudes*. Nina sighed. What had made them so lucky in love and made Nina so unlucky?

She peered through the window, then turned around and leaned against the brick wall of the building. If she didn't have love, at least she had the career she'd always wanted. She'd dreamed about this job in editorial, worked towards it since the day she'd first walked in the front doors of *Attitudes*. But now that she had it, Nina wasn't quite sure she wanted to keep it.

In truth, she thought she was out of a job until Charlotte showed up in front of her apartment building with a limo, a bouquet of roses and one of her infamous lunch reservations. She'd never seen Charlotte grovel before, but her boss managed a fair amount of humility before Nina agreed to go back to work. The fact that Cameron Ryder had finally given up his plan to buy the magazine was added to the conversation as an afterthought, with no credit given to Nina, of course. But it was that fact that rang in Nina's mind over and over again.

He'd walked away from the acquisition and she'd mysteriously been offered her job back. Nina wanted to believe he'd given it all up for her. He'd claimed he cared, but if he really cared why hadn't he called? She thought back to the last time she'd seen him, outside the elevator. Just the thought of him made her heart beat a little faster and her stomach flutter uncontrollably.

But her physical reaction to the memory of his touch was always tempered with common sense. She'd known Cameron Ryder two weeks. In that time, he'd deceived her, made love to her, and gotten her fired from her job. Just because he might have influenced her boss to rehire her didn't automatically turn him into Prince Charming.

Drawing up her courage, she yanked open the front door to Jitterbug's and walked inside. She was supposed to meet a guy in a brown tweed jacket carrying a rose. To Nina's relief, there was no one matching that description in the place. She unbuttoned her coat as she ordered her coffee, then walked to her usual table in the corner. But the moment she sat down, the memories came flooding back to her.

She remembered the night she'd met Cameron Ryder, the moment she spilled hot coffee all over his shirt and the instant their eyes locked. Nina wondered how long it would take for those memories to fade. Perhaps one date would do it, or maybe two or three. But surely five would put Cameron Ryder firmly in her past.

Over the past two weeks, there had been times when she ached to see him again. She'd always fought through the moments by summoning her pride and convincing herself that they couldn't possibly love each other. But in the deepest corners of her heart, hidden far away, was a tiny hope that someday they'd meet again. Maybe they'd run into each other on the street or maybe he'd walk into Jitterbug's. Whatever happened, in her dreams they'd look at each other and they'd both know. Just like the first time.

There had been other dreams, disjointed and disturbing, dreams that had left her feeling empty and alone. What if he'd found another woman to occupy his time? She'd never really believed he had problems getting a date. The looks that women sent his way whenever they walked down the street had disproved that theory. But a man as passionate as Cameron Ryder couldn't live like a monk forever. There would be another woman, sooner or later, and that thought brought only regret.

The bell on the door jingled and Nina looked up, holding her breath. There he was, a man in a brown tweed jacket clutching a red rose. Her first instinct was to head out the back door. But she barely had time to grab her coat before he saw her, the only woman in the place sitting alone. With a broad dimpled grin, he hurried over.

As Lizbeth had predicted, the guy had overestimated the Adonis part of the ad. Unless the Adonis he knew was slightly chubby with a receding hairline and a cherubic face that made him look all of twelve years old.

"Are you Nina?" he asked.

She forced a smile, then nodded. "You must be Edward."

"Ed," he said. He pushed the rose at her. "Wow, you're really pretty."

Her smile was so tight, Nina's face was beginning to cramp. "Thank you." She pointed to the chair across from her, but Ed quickly sat down beside her. When he'd settled, she folded her hands on the table and tried to think of something to say. "So," Nina began. "You're an artist?"

"Actually, that's just my hobby. I haven't made any money at it—yet. I work in metal sculpture, mostly copper."

"And what do you do for a living?" she asked.

"I'm a plumber," he replied.

In the midst of taking a sip of her coffee, Nina choked. Coughing, she snatched up a napkin and pressed it to her lips, smiling through watery eyes. "A—a plumber?"

"I do a lot of bathroom renovations. I specialize in period fixtures. If you've got any plumbing to be done, I'm the man for the job."

Nina couldn't help but giggle. "A plumber. That's interesting."

"I know it's not—"

"No, no. It's just that I have a special relationship with plumbing fixtures. I guess you could say we have something in common."

Though the remark seemed to relax Ed, it didn't make conversation any easier. Rather than chat, Ed preferred to simply stare at her with a moony look in his eyes. Nina nervously glanced around the coffee shop and watched as a tall man walked in the front door. At first, her heart skipped when she saw the leather jacket. Cameron had a—Nina gasped.

"Cameron," she murmured.

"What?" her date asked.

With wide eyes, Nina followed him as he strolled over to the counter and placed his order. He looked good, so tall and broad-shouldered, even more handsome than he'd been in her dreams. Her fingers clenched instinctively as her gaze dropped to his waist and then his backside. "Excuse me," she said. "I'll go get you some coffee. I'll be right back."

Without taking her eyes off Cameron, she slipped away from the table and started in the direction of the counter. He didn't notice her until she stepped to his side. And even then, he didn't seem surprised to see her. His gaze lingered on her face for a long moment. Unlike Ed's besotted stare, Nina saw true emotion behind his eyes. He smiled. "Nina," he said softly, her name like a caress she could almost feel on her skin.

She shook herself out of her brief lapse. "What are you doing here?" Nina asked, glancing frantically over at her table. Ed still watched her, his smile wide and hopeful.

"I just stopped by for coffee. I've gotten hooked on the decaf double mochas, although I've decided that I like drinking them more than wearing them."

His teasing tone warmed her blood and made her smile. But then she remembered her "date" sitting at the other table. If Cameron knew she was dating again, even if it was for work, he'd never understand. He'd think she'd given up on them and that's the last thing she wanted him to believe. "You can't stay here," she murmured.

"Why not?"

"Because—because this is my place," she replied, as if that answer was supposed to make perfect sense.

He gave her a dubious look. "Since when have you gone into the coffee business?"

"You know what I mean. I discovered this place first, so I have dibs. Now, I'd appreciate it if you'd get your coffee and leave."

Cameron grabbed his coffee, but instead of heading to the door, he turned to survey the patrons. His gaze stopped on Ed, who was now staring at the two of them. "Is that Mr. Right over there? Or should I say, Mr. Right Now?"

Nina gasped. "How did you know?"

He reached in his back pocket and pulled out his wallet. After dropping a few bills on the counter for his coffee, he took out a folded paper and handed it to her. It was the ad for "Mr. Right."

"When I first read that, I was curious as to what kind of woman would place an ad like that. Then, after I got to know you, I was a little confused." He plucked it out of her hands and carefully refolded it, tucking it into his wallet.

"The ad is part of an article I pitched to Charlotte. I'm an assistant editor now."

Cameron nodded in Ed's direction. "And he's part of the assignment?"

Nina nodded and watched as he put the ad back into his wallet. "Why did you save it?"

"As a souvenir," he said with a shrug. "You know, something to show our grandkids someday, when we tell them the story of how we met."

His words were said with such unabashed confidence that she nearly believed them herself. Her heart fluttered and her lips curled in a reluctant smile. Did he really mean what he'd said or was the teasing edge she heard in his voice a truer measure of his feelings? She glanced back at Ed. "I—I really can't talk right now. I've got this assignment and—He's a very nice man. His name is Ed."

"And what does he do?"

"He's a plumb—" She drew a sharp breath. "He's a sculptor."

Cameron grinned. "Gee, I thought you were going to say he was a plumber."

"He is that, too," Nina said, a blush warming her cheeks. "Which is a good thing. If I ever get my toe caught in a bathtub faucet or get locked in the bathroom again, at least I'll have a man who knows what to do."

"But will he know what to do afterward?" Cameron asked, his voice deep and rich, causing a shiver to skitter up her spine. "Will he know to carry you to the bed? Will he know to kiss you long and deep, until you go all soft in his arms? Will he make you moan the same way I do?"

"Did," Nina said softly. "You did make me... Past tense."

"And I will again," Cameron countered. "Future tense?"

Nina drew a shaky breath. "I really have to go now. Please leave," she said. "I can't do this if you're here."

"I haven't had my coffee yet," Cameron said.

She glanced over her shoulder. Ed was slowly pushing his chair back and he didn't look very happy. "Please," she begged.

Cameron frowned. "Tell me, Nina, are you under the impression that it's over between us?"

The question took her by surprise. Wasn't it? She didn't want it to be, but she'd spent the past two weeks convincing herself it was. Until she'd seen him walk into the coffee shop. And until she heard the sound of his voice again. Then she knew better than anyone that she couldn't stop loving Cameron Ryder. "I—I—"

Rather than listen to her stutter, he sighed impatiently, then took her face between his hands. His lips came down on hers, his tongue plundering her mouth until he'd left her breathless. And when he finally pulled away, he grinned. "It isn't over, Nina. Not by a long shot."

She drew a shaky breath, emotion pressing tears to the corners of her eyes. "I—I wish you wouldn't talk like that."

He took a step nearer. "Like what?"

"Like we have a future," she said.

His gaze fixed on hers and he looked deep into her eyes, as if he could see the truth there. "Don't we? Because that's what I want, Nina. And I hope that's what you want. I figure you'll realize that sooner or later."

Nina shook her head. "We barely know each other, Cameron. People will say it will never work."

"You don't believe in love at first sight? That when you meet Mr. Right you'll know?"

"Yes...I mean, it could happen," she said, unable to focus her thoughts with him staring into her eyes. "I just never expected it would happen to me."

"And why not?"

"Because it's a silly schoolgirl dream. When I was little, I played wedding with my Barbie dolls. And in junior high, at slumber parties, I'd put a pillowcase on my head and make a bouquet out of toilet paper flowers and pretend I was the bride. And in high school, I'd pass by a jewelry store and wonder what ring I might pick if I had any choice in the world. But that was all just a fantasy. And that's what I thought you were. A fantasy."

Nina glanced over Cam's shoulder and saw Ed approaching. He tapped Cameron on the shoulder and

Cam smiled. "Is that Ed?" he whispered, bending close so his breath tickled her ear.

Nina nodded.

"Does he look like he's going to punch me?"

Nina shook her head. "I don't think so."

Cameron stepped back and turned to Ed, then gave him a friendly smile. "I know this looks a little strange. After all, you are Nina's date, but I've got a few things to say to her. I'll only be a minute."

Ed nodded, but he refused to leave. Instead, he took a stool next to them, waiting and watching. Cameron winced, then took a step closer to Ed. He patted him on the shoulder. "You see," he said. "I really want to ask her to marry me, but with you sitting there, I'm not sure she's going to say yes."

The plumber blinked in surprise, but he wasn't half as surprised as Nina was. Ed looked at her. "Are you going to accept?"

Nina swallowed hard. Why deny it any longer? The more she tried to make sense of her feelings, the more they didn't make sense at all. She loved Cameron Ryder and nothing was going to change that. And she wanted to spend the rest of her life with him. "I'm afraid I am, Ed."

The plumber, crestfallen, could only manage a shrug before he returned to the table and retrieved his coat. Nina and Cameron watched as he left the shop, then she turned back to him. "I needed him for my story."

Cameron gently wrapped his arms around her waist, gazing down at her. "But I need you more, Nina. In all my life, I never dreamed I'd meet someone like you, someone I could love and who'd love me back.

But the moment I met you, I knew that we were meant to be together. And I think you knew it, too."

Without taking her eyes off him, she nodded. "I did know. I just didn't want to believe it."

"And do you believe it now? Do you believe that we'll love each other for the rest of our lives?"

She nodded again. Slowly, Cameron bent forward and touched his lips to hers. A tiny sigh was all she could manage before she lost herself in his kiss. Her mind spun and her heart hammered and she told herself that she'd have to wake from this dream soon. But when she opened her eyes, he was still there, holding her, needing her.

And then he pulled away and slowly dropped to one knee. He reached in his pocket and pulled out a tiny blue velvet box. "Marry me. I want to be Mr. Right Now Until Death Do Us Part."

"It's so soon," Nina said. "We've only known each other for two weeks."

"Actually, it's been four now."

Nina considered that for a moment. A slow smile curved her lips. "It has been four weeks. A month does sound a lot better than two weeks, doesn't it?"

"If it doesn't, then we'll wait two months. Or a year. Or two years. I just want to know that there's not going to be another Mr. Right in your life. I want to know that I'm the only one."

He took the ring from the box and held it out to her. With trembling fingers, she offered him her hand and he took it. The ring slipped on her finger and the diamond twinkled in the bright light of the coffee shop. "There won't be," Nina said.

He stood, then pulled her into his arms and kissed her, slowly, deeply, and so thoroughly that she never thought he'd let her go. And when he stepped back and looked down at her, Nina knew what she'd known all along: she'd gone looking for Mr. Right Now and she'd found Mr. Right.

"I think I have an ending to my article," she said.

He nuzzled her neck. "And what is that?"

"Four couples were brought together by ads in the Personal Touch. And now, in a roundabout way, it's five. Do you think Charlotte will like the little twist in the story?"

He groaned playfully. "Maybe. But I have a better ending to the story. How about the assistant editor finds love with her Internet mogul and then quits her job to help him develop his own magazine?"

"You're putting together your own magazine?" Nina asked.

Cameron nodded. "I was thinking you might be able to help since we are going to be hanging around together for the rest of our lives. I'll promise to give you a nice salary and an office with a window. And I'll remember your name. And maybe, if you're really good, you'll get to sleep with the boss."

With a laugh, Nina flung her arms around his neck and hugged him. When she'd walked away from Cameron, she thought she'd lost it all. But now, in a few short minutes, she'd found love again, and more. She'd found her future, a beautiful future with endless possibilities, a future with the man she loved, her very own Mr. Right. And she was never going to let him go.

If you enjoyed what you just read,
then we've got an offer you can't resist!

Take 2 bestselling love stories FREE!
Plus get a FREE surprise gift!

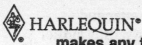

Finding Home

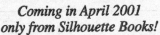
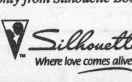

Harlequin invites you to walk down the aisle...

To honor our year long celebration of weddings, we are offering an exciting opportunity for you to own the Harlequin Bride Doll. Handcrafted in fine bisque porcelain, the wedding doll is dressed for her wedding day in a cream satin gown accented by lace trim. She carries an exquisite traditional bridal bouquet and wears a cathedral-length dotted Swiss veil. Embroidered flowers cascade down her lace overskirt to the scalloped hemline; underneath all is a multi-layered crinoline.

Join us in our celebration of weddings by sending away for your own Harlequin Bride Doll. This doll regularly retails for $74.95 U.S./approx. $108.68 CDN. One doll per household. Requests must be received no later than June 30, 2001. Offer good while quantities of gifts last. Please allow 6-8 weeks for delivery. Offer good in the U.S. and Canada only. Become part of this exciting offer!

Simply complete the order form and mail to:
"A Walk Down the Aisle"

IN U.S.A	IN CANADA
P.O. Box 9057	P.O. Box 622
3010 Walden Ave.	Fort Erie, Ontario
Buffalo, NY 14240-9057	L2A 5X3

Enclosed are eight (8) proofs of purchase found on the last page of every specially marked Harlequin series book and $3.75 check or money order (for postage and handling). Please send my Harlequin Bride Doll to:

_____

Name (PLEASE PRINT)

_____

Address   Apt. #

_____

City   State/Prov.   Zip/Postal Code

_____

Account # (if applicable)   **098 KIK DAEW**

HARLEQUIN®
Makes any time special ®

Visit us at www.eHarlequin.com

A Walk Down the Aisle
Free Bride Doll Offer
One Proof-of-Purchase

PHWDAPOP